A THOUSAND YEARS IN A NIGHT . . . ?

Sieur Bohun de Freitas supposed it had to be true—that he had gone to sleep and woken up a thousand years later. There was so much that was outlandish—those lightly clad wenches hidden in the box his "hosts" called "the three-vee" were mighty fetching, though he had not found a way to get them out from behind the glass screen to where he could enjoy them.

Suddenly a gaggle of his captors invaded his quarters and pushed a slack-bodied fellow at him. "This is your distant grandson, Mon Sieur, Harold Freitas. It is thanks to him that you have been fetched across time—"

"Did you say Harold?" For a loyal liege of William of Normandy there could only be one response to that hated name. Bohun snarled and launched himself at his visitor. He had no weapons, but bare hands would be enough!

TIMESCOOP

JOHN BRUNNER

A DELL BOOK

Published by
Dell Publishing Co., Inc.
1 Dag Hammarskjold Plaza
New York, New York 10017

ISBN: 0-440-18916-0

Printed in the United States of America
Previous Dell edition
One printing
New Dell edition
First printing—January 1981

"Each in his narrow cell forever laid
The rude forefathers of the hamlet sleep."

—Gray: *An Elegy Written in a Country Churchyard*

TIMESCOOP

CHAPTER I

"That'll do nicely, Chester," said Harold Freitas III as the statue drew abreast of the long lounge on which his wife, Sarah, was reclining. The calm-faced, rather good-looking young Negro who had volunteered to push it on its hissing air-pallet from the door of the elevator cut the power and it sank to the floor with a solid-marble thunk.

"There!" Harold added to Sarah. "What do you think of that?"

Lithe and exquisite as usual, Sarah swung her bare golden legs to the floor and shook back her shoulder-long fair hair. There was a long pause. During it, Harold realized that, if only the big breakthrough had happened on a Friday, he would have been able to tell her the news at their country place in Arizona, and in some indefinable sense that would have been infinitely more appropriate.

But it was Wednesday, so they were in the Los Angeles penthouse, a place so completely of the twenty-first century its very walls seemed to exclude even thoughts of the dead past. He felt the first twinge of apprehension lest his carefully planned surprise should go to waste through such a silly accident.

I ought to have waited to Friday evening after all.

But there were two good reasons why he couldn't have. For one thing, ever since their marriage he had felt a trifle uncomfortable in Sarah's presence. He felt, in some way he could never pin down, inferior to her—not that anyone could have accused her of acting as though that were her view of him, not that any outsider could have detected friction between them. He simply seemed to lack the ability to impress her, and surely after five years a man ought to have done at least one thing to impress his wife!

And for another thing, he was purely bursting with need to share the news with somebody.

At least, he noted, she was taking the trouble to get up and walk around the statue to inspect it from all sides, to touch it here and there with a probing finger, to stand back with folded arms and give a nod.

"The *Hermes* of Praxiteles," she said. "And rather a good copy, if I'm any judge."

"No!" Harold said in triumph. "Not a copy—that's exactly the point.

She gazed at him blankly for a moment. Then she gave her high tinkling laugh. "Oh, Harold! You're not going to tell me somebody conned you into buying this as the original? The original is in the museum at Olympia—I've seen it there. It couldn't be for sale by any stretch of the imagination, and I don't suppose it could possibly be stolen, either. Besides, it shows more than a few signs of old age. I mean it's chipped!"

"That," said Harold doggedly," is the *Hermes* of Praxiteles. Not a copy but the original. We finally got the bugs out of the Timescoop project, and this is the first object larger than a clay pot that we've brought forward with it. The power alone cost us about half a million."

At least, he reflected with grim satisfaction, if he hadn't impressed her he'd bewildered her, and that was a new sensation. She glanced in astonishment from him to the statue, then to Chester, and back to him.

"I don't think I quite understand," she said.

He was tempted to say that, if she took more interest in her husband's work, she'd have known about the project from the beginning and would understand perfectly. Conscience held back the words; he himself understood only a fraction of what the Freitas billions had rendered possible. It was hard to have been made, at the age of twenty-nine, what a commentator over K3V-*Fortune* had termed "the rider on the wild horse"—in other words, to have been dropped into the saddle of Freitas Interplanetary at a time when the sheer financial inertia of the corporation implied that no single man, president or humble clerk, could hope to do more than divert the dozens of individual research projects and public-service enterprises within the empire by a degree or two of arc from their preplanned courses.

He turned away grumpily to serve himself a drink from the liquor console. "You'd better ask Chester for the details," he threw over his shoulder. "He's the man who takes the credit for all this."

"Well now, that's a bit of an exaggeration," Chester Waley said in a mild tone. "It certainly could never have succeeded without the twenty or thirty people on our team, and above all, it couldn't have come off without the help of Sparky."

"Maybe not," Harold said, and essayed a mild witticism. "But one can hardly invite a computer to dinner, can one?"

The moment the words were out of his mouth, he felt the joke wasn't really very funny. Sparky—SPARCI, Self-Programming Automatic Rapid Computer and Integrator—was even higher on the list of people who disturbed him and made him feel inadequate than Sarah was. Nobody ever referred to Sparky as "it," only as "he," and he was such an integral part of the Freitas Interplanetary setup that it was a jolt to remember where the calm friendly voice over the office intercom was coming from.

"Drinks?" Harold said to cover the flatness of his last remark. "For you, darling?"

Sarah returned to her lounge and composed her graceful limbs into a decorative posture; she was wearing a high-fashion tabard in Freitas syntholon, reaching from shoulder to crotch and designed so that it never *quite* revealed the intimate details of her anatomy to which it so carefully directed the eye by the curves it fell into. She said, "Not for me, thank you. If Chester is going to tell me about something technical, I shall need all my faculties to follow him. You know I haven't got a scientific mind."

The Negro made a disclamatory gesture. "On the other hand, Mrs Freitas, I believe you have a far greater appreciation of history than someone like myself. And art and literature, of course."

Sarah shrugged. "Oh, the past is dead, so it just lies there and doesn't jerk around when you try to examine it closely."

"But that's exactly the point!" Harold said, spinning away from the liquor console to face her again and contriving to slop over the back of his hand an ounce or two of the drink he had taken over. He kept his curses silent and went on, "The past needn't be dead—not any more. Look, this statue *is* the original! Or to be exact, it's a cross section of the original, one chronon deep, allowed to expand in the present into a facsimile of its full four-dimensional structure. You see . . ."

His voice trailed away as it became clear that Sarah did not see, and the sneaking suspicion arose in his mind that she was being willfully obtuse because it was he who was giving her the explanation. He knew it was the right one, because he was quoting word for word a summary issued by Sparky.

"You have a go, Chester," he sighed, and carried his drink to an inflatable armchair on the other side of the room.

"I'll do my best," Chester said, and likewise sat down, leaning forward with elbows on knees. "It is a bit difficult to grasp at first, Mrs Freitas, but I think I can convey the fundamental concept. Have you ever thought that an instantaneous object could not exist?"

Sarah pondered for a moment. Then she nodded. "You mean in the perceptual sense?"

"Precisely. Therefore, as well as length, breadth and height, an object must possess duration. Just as there is a minimum spatial length—usually taken as the diameter of an electron because we still can't observe events occurring in a smaller compass—there is also a minimum temporal length. Now suppose you were able to cut through some object with an infinitesimally fine wire, one electron's diameter in thickness—do you think that would perceptibly affect the object?"

Sarah pondered again, and finally shook her head.

"Effectively it wouldn't," Chester agreed. "It might just possibly alter the total electrical potential of the object by ionizing a few of its molecules, but the odds are all against it. But cutting a one-chronon cross section of an object is a different matter. All the constituent particles of that object are sliced through by the cut; in other words, there's a hiatus in its duration."

"What causes it to resume when the other side of the cut is reached?" Sarah demanded, and Harold gave her a startled and irritated glare. If she could ask that acute a question after such a skimpy introduction to the subject, then she was deliberately snubbing him. She must understand very clearly.

"It doesn't resume," Chester said. "It exists, in a four-dimensional sense, both sides of the cut. But because the cross section is timeless, it having no time to exist in owing to the conditions established to make it possible at all, it makes no difference where the cross section is then transported.

"What we've done at Timescoop is to—ah—*constrain* such cross sections to the present. Then it does become technical; you have to derive information from a theoretically information-free environment and feed in power to permit the forward duration of the item to resume, and so on. But right here, in the shape of this statue, is proof that it can be done, and even though we saw it—uh—*grow* in the Timescoop lab this morning, it is in every possible respect the original which we located in Praxiteles's own workshop and cross-sectioned just before its dispatch to the temple it was commissioned for."

"I see," nodded Sarah. "In other words, so far as an outsider like me is concerned, it's a fake."

CHAPTER II

There followed a few seconds of tense silence. Harold broke it by jumping to his feet.

"No! *Not* a fake! Chester just told you—"

"Oh, Harold, really," Sarah said in that tone of weary and almost patronizing patience which he had come to know so well since they got married. "The *Hermes* of Praxiteles is—I forget exactly how old, but certainly two or three thousand. If that thing there is fresh from the workshop, it's not the original. What would an archeologist report if you asked him to check on the stone that thing's carved from?"

Harold's jaw dropped and stayed dropped. Even the normally imperturbable Chester blinked rapidly several times.

"Mrs Freitas has a very good point there," he murmured.

"Thank you," Sarah said. "Do you get what I'm driving at, Harold? In 2065 the stone is fresh-cut, not aged or weathered; it hasn't been handled by sightseers who've left a deposit of—of finger grease, I suppose—on the original, and given it the patina of the ages."

"But it *is* the original," Harold insisted obstinately.

"In your sense, perhaps. Not in a collector's sense, or an art historian's. What were you thinking of doing with this Timescoop of yours?"

"Why—uh . . ." Harold stumble-tongued. Chester came sympathetically to the rescue.

"Well, it's going to be announced to the public shortly, Mrs Freitas—so far we've been lucky with our security and we believe no one else has even the remotest inkling of our success. It'll naturally take a while yet, about six or eight months according to Sparky's projections, before we can rely on perfect operation every time. There are so many incidentals to sort out, like the fine-focusing technique we use to make sure we get what we're after and not half or something which happened to be standing next to it. As yet, that's dreadfully slow; it took us all of nine weeks to set up the *Hermes* job. We need to get it down to a matter of hours before the technique becomes economic."

"In what sense economic? How do you price objects dragged out of the past?"

Listening, Harold felt himself trembling on the edge of a gulf of disaster. This was by far the most hopeful thing that had happened since he found himself tossed into the presidential chair of Freitas Interplanetary following the death of his father, Harold Freitas II, on the way back from Mars—the victim of a meteor strike. And here was Sarah not merely failing to be impressed but actually undermining this fantastic achievement with idiotic grumbles!

He said harshly, "It's all been costed, of course. By Sparky. I told you, the power required to bring your—your *present* from the *past* cost about half a million. But what do you suppose the market price of that statue would be if it were to be offered for sale? Ten times that at the least! And one wouldn't have to stick to such massive objects; that simply happened to be one whose precise location on a precise date in the past could conveniently be established. For about a hundred and twenty thousand we can bring forward the *Mona Lisa*—"

"I'll bid a buck for it," Sarah cut in.

"Oh, stop talking nonsense!"

"I'm not talking nonsense." Sarah jumped up and went to fetch herself a drink, after all. Belatedly, when she glanced a question at Chester, Harold realized he hadn't offered a drink to their visitor, and since the visitor nodded and smiled, he obviously wanted one. Christ, wasn't anything going right today?

"You say Sparky costed this project's economic viability," Sarah continued as she attended to the controls on the console. "Well, all I can say is that he's an ignorant idiot. Look, Harold, I'm sure you went to a lot of trouble to be able to give me that statue this evening, but you wasted the corporation's money, you know. For a hundred thousand you could have hired the right mineralogists to match the marble, the right technicians to take measurements accurate to a few microns off the original in the museum, and a competent hack sculptor to reproduce them.

You spent five times as much and all you've wound up with is—regardless of what you say—a duplicate."

Chester was looking very grave. He said diffidently, "I'd be inclined to take what your wife says seriously, Mr Freitas. It's not my field, but I do have the impression that it's only the scarcity value which keeps up the prices of works of art—"

"Yes, of course it is!" Harold snapped. "Our plan is designed to maintain scarcity value, not destroy it. If we were to scoop the *Mona Lisa,* you think we'd do it a dozen times over? Not at all. We plan to make the announcement, mount a major publicity campaign, and invite tenders from museums and private collectors for whatever they most desperately want. The highest bids will get our first attention. And it's not just works of art, but archeological relics and important documents and lost historical data generally that we plan to get hold of. And one and only one client will get the benefit, the highest bidder. He'll also get a watertight contract assuring him that we will never repeat the assignment we accepted from him."

"And how long after you announce your discovery will you retain a monopoly?" Sarah demanded in an icy tone. "What's to stop some unscrupulous bastard setting up his own operation?"

"Well, this isn't exactly the kind of technique one man in a basement can—" Harold began. She cut him short.

"Harold, right over there behind that nice smart hammered-gold panel there's a keyboard which gives you or me or anyone access to computing capacity that only giant corporations disposed of a generation ago. All the wealth of the Roman Empire couldn't have bought Nero a three-vee set—if it could have, maybe he wouldn't have been so bored he needed to burn Christians! If I were the curator of an art gallery, say, faced with an offer like yours, I'd estimate how long it would be before every hole-in-the-corner little rival of mine could boast the same exhibits with the same kind of warranty of genuineness and I'd halve my original bid and then halve it again because all I was getting was a nine-days' wonder."

Harold had gone very pale, but in his heart he knew she was right.

"In short," she wound up, "the operation isn't going to persuade people to pay for the mere power you say it takes to bring it off, let alone amortize the billions you've probably spent on research."

"Now just a second!" Harold objected. "Think of all the damaged works of art that people would like to have complete—think of the *Venus di Milo!* Think of the archeological relics which were robbed before scientists could get to investigate them, like the burial treasures of the Pharaohs which were stolen from the Pyramids! You're not going to tell me that people wouldn't like to have those—and we can get them. In fact, the Pyramids are a very easy target because they can be pinpointed exactly."

"But pure knowledge doesn't command a particularly high market price," Chester said regretfully. "I was in college with a friend who wanted desperately to know whether it was true that Peter the Great, Ivan the Terrible, Napoleon and Henry VIII were, as the medical historians allege, really afflicted with syphilis. I'm sure he still wants to know that, and the Timescoop technique could enable him to find out. But he's teaching in a small African college right now, and the annual budget for his department would be swallowed up by a day's operation of the Timescoop itself."

"This is exactly the kind of thing we want to be able to do for people," Harold said. "Solve the riddles of history. But until we've made the operation self-supporting, which means, of course, we are going to have to amortize our investment, we shan't be able to afford these luxury frills."

"Well, if you think you're going to pay for them by—ah—*importing* duplicates of existing works of art and expecting them to maintain their market value, you're wrong," Sarah said flatly. She rose from the lounge, setting aside her empty glass. "I programmed dinner for about this time—shall we see if it's ready?"

But her remark fell on deaf ears. Harold was gazing at Chester in wonderment.

"Did you say the Timescoop would enable your friend to find out about all these historical characters suffering from syphilis?"

"Ah—in principle, I guess it could," Chester agreed cautiously.

"You mean there's nothing to stop you from bringing forward a—what's your word?—a cross section of a *living human being?*"

"We never tested it out." Chester shrugged. "But since the cross section itself is by definition timeless, and once the power is supplied to it in the present to enable it to resume its normal forward progression into time, it's indistinguishable from the original, I see no theoretical objection."

"Then that's what we'll do," Harold declared triumphantly.

"What? You mean—oh—send for Shakespeare and rent him out to universities at a million dollars a day?" Sarah said. "Harold, be reasonable. I think this thing has turned your brain. Nobody will ever believe you didn't simply hire an actor and reprogram his memories, not unless you make public every detail of the Timescoop technique so that people who don't have to worry about amortizing the research investment can climb on your shoulders and offer the same service for the mere cost of the power."

"They'll believe me, all right," Harold said, rising to his feet and puffing out his chest. The whole scheme had come clear to his mind in seconds. "Sarah, do you know what next year is?"

"Would you like me to fetch you a calendar?" she said with sarcastic sweetness.

"I'm not in the mood for jokes!" he blazed.

"Well, of course I do!" She stared at him in surprise, as though taken aback by the violence of his last outburst.

"Then since you're so interested in history, you must know what it will be the thousandth anniversary of?"

"2066? The Norman conquest of England!"

"Precisely." Harold turned to Chester with a sketch for a bow. "I don't usually talk much about this, Chester, because my grandfather dinned it into me as a child that it doesn't make any difference who you're descended from unless you can do something yourself to match what your ancestors did to gain their own notoriety. He certainly did that, by founding Freitas Interplanetary. I'm sure, but for his tragic accident, my father would also have made his personal mark on history.

"The fact stands, though, that I come from an old and distinguished family with far more than its proper share of outstanding personalities. I'm proud of that in the same way as I'm proud to have inherited Freitas Interplanetary. For example, the Sieur Bohun de Freitas held land under William the First of England, and is listed in the *Domesday Book.* Ah—Sir Godwin de Freitas-Molyneux was a notable figure at the time of the Crusades, and was killed storming the walls of the Holy City after leading a famous charge at the battle of Acre. A distant connection, not in the direct line, is reputed to have taught navigation to Amerigo Vespucci. In Colonial days in this country, Reverend Ebenezer Freitas was a pillar of New England society, and there are streets named after him in at least three Massachusetts towns. And so on." He made an all-embracing gesture.

"This is how we're going to celebrate the announcement of Timescoop to the public, and if it doesn't fire the world's imagination, then nothing in the universe will do so. We're going to have a Freitas family reunion, and it's not going to be some piddling little get-together of cousins and nephews and nieces at the spot on the Ould Sod where great-grandad shared a patch of straw with the pigs!

"No, the Freitas reunion is going to be unique, and—and oh boy! Is this ever going to make the Mellons and the Kennedys and the Schatzenheims look *sick!*"

CHAPTER III

"Can it be done?" Harold Freitas said to the twenty-one images of scientists, administrative staff and PR men occupying the screen-band facing his desk: all faces natural size, all at his own eye height as he sat behind his barricade of communications and data-processing equipment. This was the office from which his grandfather had directed the corporation; settling into the deeply padded genuine leather chair he had inherited without warning gave him new assurance, new proof of his identity among the teeming billions of Earth.

And this, at long last, was an idea of his own. He had been prompted to it, but no one had actually brought it along on a platter and invited him to take the credit, which was what usually happened. He almost glanced at Chester Waley, but prevented himself.

"Sparky thinks so," came the reluctant answer at long last from James Quentin, vice-president in charge of research: a tired-looking man in his fifties, with untidy gray hair which, out of inverted vanity, he refused to have dyed.

"Sparky thought we could finance the Timescoop program by offering works of art," Harold said. "Sparky was wrong."

"I beg your pardon, Mr Freitas," said a mild voice from the speaker underneath the only one of the screens which bore a fixed, rather than a mobile image. The picture on it was of a smiling rigid face: the death mask of Voltaire. Sarah had chosen it to replace the original cartoon-sketch character his grandfather had been satisfied with, he being old enough to remember the Magic Piano from his childhood. Every time Harold looked at it it gave him the creeps.

"I gave the answer I was asked for," the computer continued. "I was asked to estimate the cost of bringing forward from the past certain masterpieces included in a list appended to the question. I did so. It is not my fault if someone jumped to a hasty conclusion because those costings were so far below the present artificially inflated prices obtained at art auctions."

"Never mind recriminations," said Louisa Fold, vice-president in charge of public relations: a striking woman in her early forties, with the complexion and figure of a much younger girl and the devious mind of a cobra winding up to strike. "Myself, I like the proposal very much. I ran a few preliminary analyses before coming to this conference, and all of them were favorable. One factor which invariably operates in the case of a family reunion is that in the modern world most people feel slightly dissociated from their environment. They strike out on their own at an early age because they feel oppressed and limited by parental directives, but within only a few years—ten at most—they become aware of their own insecurity and develop a sneaking envy for families like the Schatzenheims who can afford to bring their outlying members together for a grand celebration. And above all, they envy those who organize such a reunion because they are the ones to whom the rest of the relatives feel indebted."

Harold scowled. He almost always did when the Schatzenheims were mentioned. Four-S—Schatzenheim Solar System Services—and Freitas Interplanetary enjoyed more or less the same kind of uneasy accommodation as, say, Ford and General Motors had done during the previous century: both giants, neither able to exterminate the other, yet both unspeakably jealous. With a colossal flourish of trumpets, the current head of the Schatzenheim dynasty, Solomon, had held a family runion in 2050, for which he brought back at his own expense nearly eight hundred relatives from places as far away as the Pluto orbital survey station, and built an automated university on the spot in Poland from which, in the 1880s, their common ancestor, David Schatzenheim, had set off with his wife and nine children on the wanderings which had climaxed in New York's garment district. The family home had long vanished, but the neo-Communist Polish government had been very pleased indeed to accept the offer of the university in place of the blocks of twentieth-century flats that had been built on the site; they had been thrown up all anyhow during the population explosion of the eighties and were showing their age.

"If I may continue," Louisa Fold said, continuing, "I'd like to draw your attention to a rather interesting point I turned up during my first inquiries. Expressed as a percentage of English-language publicity media available for it, the story of the celebrated Mellon reunion nearly a century ago enjoyed something like a decimal oh-oh-oh-one return. Curiously enough, the Schatzenheim reunion on a similar scale—*mutatis mutandis,* naturally—secured better than an oh-oh-oh-three return. But whereas the Mellon reunion registered a Gayton durability of only two-five-seven, the Schatzenheim reunion is still registering three-nine-two, fifteen years later."

"There are several of us," said Quentin irritably, "who don't understand Miss Fold's jargon."

"What it boils down to," Louisa said, "is that, because of the changing nature of our society, the Schatzenheim reunion stuck in many more people's minds for a much longer time and doubtless has had great influence on, for instance, their success in advertising. All the factors I can evaluate tend to the conclusion that, if there were to be a Freitas reunion involving a major new scientific breakthrough, it would create unprecedented Gayton readings for the event, perhaps even approaching the theoretical impossibility of unity, which represents awareness by every adult member of the linguistic group concerned of all the minor details one year or more after the news reports ceased to appear."

"In other words," Harold suggested, "it would be the biggest publicity gimmick of the century."

"Perhaps of all time," Louisa said smugly, and sat back in her chair.

"That's settled, then," Harold said. "The Timescoop news is to be kept under strictest security wraps until it is possible to break it in conjunction with a grand reunion of my ancestors. I'd like the target date to be January first next year owing to the associations with the thousandth anniversary of the Norman Conquest. Chester?"

"As near as we can judge, that would be about right,"

Chester said. "We've had considerable success with inanimate objects now, and providing we can run a few tests on human beings beforehand to make certain our guess about their ability to survive is well founded, we shall be ready some time around then."

"Good! But I guess we'd better have a backstop date as well. Any ideas?"

"Old Christmas Day," Louisa said. "Sixth January. And for long-distance purposes, the spring equinox in March."

"Sparky?" Harold said.

The computer could not nod the image in its screen, but he had the impression it would have done so had it been equipped. He made a mental note to get rid of the Voltaire mask and substitute something more congenial, perhaps an animated construct face.

"Both the suggested backstop dates have apt mental associations among the public. And it is probable that only the former would have to be used."

"Okay," Harold said. "Now I want a preliminary rundown on all the associated problems. If we're going to bring people here from the past, for example, we shall need to accommodate them; we shall need in some cases, no doubt, to teach them modern colloquial English." He hoped it didn't sound as though he was quoting Sarah, which in fact he was—these points were some of the many she had raised in argument with him to try and persuade him not to stick with his plan. But he'd been adamant. Louisa's favorable opinion had merely made him more determined than ever.

Still, these were valid problems which any rational person would have had to take into account.

"And then there are the medical problems," Chester murmured. "It's known that germs undergo mutation far more rapidly than larger creatures; suppose one of these ancestors turns out to have a variety of flu we don't possess automatic immunity to?"

"Oh, that's a minor difficulty," said Helen Whymore, the vice-president in charge of personnel welfare. She made a dismissing gesture with one beautifully manicured hand. "We've been dealing for years with the rehabilitation of sick spacemen, and nothing picked up on Earth could pose the problems we meet when someone comes home with a load of Martian eczema, for example."

She leaned closer to the camera at her end, enlarging her face on the screens.

"The cultural problems, now—those could really be tricky! I'll circulate a memo about this later, but I'm immediately struck by the possibility that there might be the risk of shock, especially among people from the far past to whom the fundamental concepts of modern life are completely alien. At what point are you planning to—ah—*pick up* the subjects?"

"It largely depends on whether we can definitely establish their whereabouts at a convenient moment," Chester replied. "But in general, it looks as though it will be while they're asleep—it's frequently pretty easy to determine that such and such a notable person slept the night of such a date in the blue room in the north wing of the mansion, or whatever."

"Now there's exactly the kind of difficulty I'm warning you against," Helen said. "You don't want them thinking that their twenty-first-century experiences are all a dream, do you?"

She waited a second until she was sure everyone had absorbed her point, then repeated, "But I'll circulate a memo about this when I've had time to digest the idea."

Harold was extremely relieved that she wasn't going to pursue the matter further; every time he himself thought about it, he kept coming up with fresh objections. Nonetheless, he was damned well going to see this project through, come hell or high water.

He said loudly, "Thank you, Helen, that's just the kind of problem we want people to bring to our notice before we start the operation. It's not insoluble by any means, though. Remember, we can call on some of the best talent in the world to cope with these side effects, and since we already have a clear head start on the main problem, I fully expect we shall deal with the subsidiary ones without excessive delay. Thank you all very much and I look forward to receiving your various memos on the subject in the next day or two."

Directly he had cut the conference connection, he punched for a circuit to the genealogical research bureau he had retained to investigate his ancestry. To the auto-clerk who took his call he said, "Mr Flannagan, please!"

And when, a moment later, Flannagan's stage-Irish face appeared, red-nosed and knobbly like a potato, he said, "Do you have any recommendations for me yet, Mr Flannagan?"

"Ah, Mr Freitas!" The genealogist smiled. "Yes, sir, we most definitely do. Seldom in all my half-century of experience have I had the pleasure of investigating such a distinguished heredity, not even when I was retained as a rather unwilling junior director on the Schatzenheim reunion program fifteen years ago. We have clear documentary evidence of descent for a thousand years at the least, and we may well be able to push the limits back still further."

"A thousand will do very well," Harold said. "What I want to know is, who are the ten or so most distinguished among the distinguished, and is there any point in their lives at which you can pin them down to within a few yards?"

He was aware as he spoke that, if someone with the right information had been listening, that would have been the end of all secrecy on the Timescoop project. But the circuit was sealed automatically; he had once been told that as many clients consulted the genealogical research bureau to disguise a family scandal as to discover their notable forebears, and he was prepared to believe it.

"That assignment will take a little longer than you have as yet accorded us," said Flannagan. "And," he added diffidently, "it may prove rather costly."

"The hell with the cost," Harold said. "Just get me the data."

CHAPTER IV

"There is to be a family reunion of the Freitas clan," whispered Cy Detrick. He was a very lowly cog in the enormous interlocking machine of the Freitas Interplanetary corporation, but he was the one who had managed to secure an interrogation code for Sparky and sell his knowledge to the Four-S intelligence service. Not that the code gave him access to the deep-level data banks, but it was better than nothing and the Schatzenheims had been grateful for his assistance to the tune of nearly fifty thousand dollars over the past five years.

"Thank you," said the anonymous voice at the other end of the phone.

"So once again the Freitas kid fails to come up with an *original* idea," Solomon Schatzenheim rumbled across the breakfast table at which he received the news. "Hah! Copying a notion to gain publicity which we used fifteen years ago!"

"And which other wealthy families had worn to shreds a century before that," said his current wife, Miriam, from the other side of the row of silver-plated dishes holding kedgeree, deviled kidneys, curried eggs, sausages and the other proper appurtenances of the traditional British country-house breakfast which were always put out in the mornings for Solomon and his spouse of the moment. *He* never touched them—if he ate anything apart from a poppyseed roll, he sent to the kitchens for gefilte fish.

"What is worse," Miriam continued as she selected another segment of smoked haddock from the yellow pile of the kedgeree on her plate, "the best you could manage was to drag everybody back to some miserable hamlet in the middle of Poland surrounded with collective farms and ugly concrete apartment blocks, whereas anyone bearing the Freitas name can probably trace his descent back to somewhere romantic, like a Viking castle or at the least a fortified manor house with a moat around it."

Solomon narrowed his deep-set eyes. He was in his late sixties, but he was in no sense an elderly man; he was of a lean, fine-drawn build with a hawk nose and a sharp, determined chin. He said, "And what makes you think it's so much better to ride on the back of your ancestors than to pull yourself up out of the mud by your own bootstraps?"

"The fact that you couldn't show your family was successful beyond—what was it?—1890 or so, I think. There's a big difference between that and 1066."

"Are you trying to annoy me?" Solomon said in a low, dangerous tone.

"Yes." Miriam pushed aside her plate and reached for her coffee cup. "I have to admit that, when I married into the Schatzenheims, I never expected to find such a positively Moslem attitude toward women as you have. I'm doing my best to goad you past the point at which you can any longer put up with me."

She tapped a cigarette out of the dispenser box on the table, set it to her fractionally too thin lips, and drew on it, let gray smoke wreathe from her aristocratically fine nostrils, and bared her shining white teeth in a mocking parody of a smile. It reached no farther up her face than her cheekbones.

"Then you're going about it the wrong way," Solomon said with composure. "Even in the short time we've spent together, you should have realized that you've adopted the worst possible means of inducing me to surrender. You are a very beautiful woman, you are half my age, and in spite of the fact that you have as yet contrived not to bear me any children, you are impressively fertile. In short, you are in all respects a very suitable wife for the head of the Schatzenheim family."

"But a very poor mother for the *next* generation of the Schatzenheims," Miriam said quietly. "I simply don't like you, Solomon. I wish I did. But I think you're a pompous bore, and whatever you may know about being the head of a major corporation, you know from absolutely damn *all* about being a husband, let alone a father. Why in hell don't you just turn me loose and give me some reasonable allowance, say a couple of thousand bucks a week, and find yourself some nice little Jewish cow eager to breed her kind by the dozen?"

She saw the muscles tense as his hand trembled near the smoking-hot dish in which reposed the deviled kidneys, and added, "Sure, go on—throw them at me! If you hit me in the face, I'll take my burns straight down to Mount Sinai Hospital and all the news services will be right there in the ward when they're putting on the bandages!"

Later, in the New York headquarters of the Four-S Corporation—which for sentimental reasons occupied the ground once dominated by a successful early twentieth-century garment firm—Solomon Schatzenheim digested his fury in the quiet ancient manner and, in a tone that milk could not have surpassed for mildness, put a series of questions to various subordinates who specialized in Four-S's relations with its rivals.

Freitas himself might be a kid. His grandfather, though, who was almost of Solomon's own generation and who had died so young as to make Solomon occasionally uneasy, had been a tougher customer entirely, and enough of his legacy had survived in Freitas Interplanetary to make the gathering of commercial intelligence within the corporation both difficult and expensive.

All the authoritative opinions that converged on his office today, whether from human personnel or from computerized analyses, suggested that the idea of holding a family reunion to gain publicity would result in a lead balloon.

Yet and still, there was the permanent snag: Freitas's internal security was streets ahead of anyone else's. Every day recent decisions taken by the directorate of Solar Mexican were fed to the Four-S computers for evaluation; every other day, or thereabouts, data came trickling in from Sovcomp or from the Mao Coordinating Institute for Planning or from All-India Enterprises, and Four-S kept its head above water in consequence.

Harold Freitas I, though, must have been practically paranoid to maintain such tight security within the company! And though since his death there had been one or two minor slip-ups, nothing had come along to offer a really useful breach in the defenses.

Merely repeating what had been done over and over was so plainly a pointless waste of time and money that Solomon's suspicions were aroused. Certainly Freitas didn't lack computing facilities; indeed, they said that Sparky was among the world's finest data-processing machines.

So what extra factor had crept into the equation unnoticed?

Suddenly he was gripped by the determination to get to the bottom of this mystery. He issued a blanket authorization to go the limit in bribes and subverting double agents at any point where Freitas was concerned.

But even as he leaned back in his chair after giving the order, he wondered gloomily whether it was enough.

Left at home as usual during the greater part of the day, Miriam Schatzenheim grew more and more bored. She'd had her face done the day before; she'd had her hair done the day before that and the coiffeur had warned her against having it done more than once a week because it was so fine and liable to split; she'd been shopping on both days during the afternoon and she was running out of things she wanted and also out of her personal credit—Solomon was strict in limiting her to a thousand a week.

Also there were more unworn clothes in the wardrobe than she had engagements lined up to display them at.

So that, as usual, drove her eventually to the phone to idle away an hour or two before lunch in gossiping with her friends. Leafing through the directory of most-used numbers which the phone automatically projected on her screen at the touch of a button, she had a sudden inspiration. It was a long while since she had spoken to Sarah Freitas.

And she rather liked Sarah, though it would hardly have been politic to cultivate a close friendship with her. She felt that they both had much the same kind of trouble with their husbands, having married more into a corporation than into a family.

Besides, it would annoy Solomon if he found out, and she could take steps to make it *when* rather than *if*.

Chuckling quietly, she punched the Freitas code, across the continent in Los Angeles.

"Well!" Sarah said in astonishment as she recognized the striking dark face in the phone screen. "How nice of you to call up, Miriam. It's been a long time, hasn't it?"

"About a year," Miriam said. "Since that Midsummer Ball you held at the Grand Canyon."

"Is it really that long?" Sarah shook her head. "How time does fly, doesn't it? How have you been?"

"Not so good," Miriam said, sighing. "Oh, I don't mean I've been ill or anything, but life's just been generally flat."

"I know exactly what you mean," Sarah agreed.

"Yes, I thought you would. Do you ever get the feeling you're married to a huge anonymous organization and not to a proper husband?"

"Not quite," Sarah said after a moment's consideration. "My Harold is really an awfully sweet person, and one must admit it was terribly hard on him suddenly to be thrust into the presidential chair without the proper training and experience, so I suppose he's kind of got into the habit of compromising and accepting other people's expert opinions. Which, of course, is hardly the right way to run a marriage—I mean in the sense that he tends to look to me all the time to make our domestic decisions for him."

"To me that sounds like paradise," Miriam countered. "If I get a look-in on something concerning Solomon and me, it's generally because he's too preoccupied with one of his big business deals to care about having the last word on something so relatively unimportant in his eyes."

"You poor dear," Sarah said with sympathy.

"I guess you might say he doesn't think of his wives as people," Miriam continued. "I heard pretty much the same from his last wife, Abigail—but after, not before, I said I'd marry him. Mainly I'm his wife because I look right and have the proper social graces. What's happened to men this century, Sarah? Aren't there any left who know how to give a woman what she wants—who know how to woo her and keep her happy with little compliments and surprises?"

Sarah looked past the phone to the statue, which as yet she had not made up her mind what to do about. It was a very splendid object in itself, regardless of whether it was called a "fake" or an "original," but in the context of the Los Angeles penthouse it was subtly wrong. And either it would have to be transferred to the Arizona place, or else the apartment would have to be done over completely in Neo-Grecian Classical to make it seem right. She was half-minded to choose the latter and more expensive course—moreover, the far more inconvenient course, for it would involve their moving to a hotel or somewhere while the decorators were at work—just to teach Harold a little lesson.

"Is something wrong?" Miriam inquired from the phone.

"Oh, no! Sorry, my mind wandered for a moment," Sarah said.

They talked on for a few minutes longer, ending the chat with an insincere promise to get together for a drink when they were next on the same coast at the same time, and Miriam cut the circuit.

For a long time after the screen blanked, Sarah sat with eyes unfocused, contemplating the idea which had been planted in her mind.

Perhaps it was true that something had gone out of twenty-first-century men. Perhaps this ridiculous notion of Harold's about reuniting his ancestors in the present wasn't such a stupid plan, after all. Perhaps way back when, there had been real guts and determination in his family heritage.

She suddenly realized she was looking forward to finding out.

CHAPTER V

"Mr Flannagan," Harold said, "this is Dr Chester Waley. I've asked him to sit in on this discussion by phone for technical reasons which I won't bother you with. Just take it from me that there may be certain crucial questions he needs to ask you in connection with the establishment of my precise genealogy."

Flannagan nodded a polite greeting at the image in the screen on the far side of the office. He said, "Ah! You have a very interesting physiognomy, Dr Waley! One can see at a glance that you mingle probably a Castilian strain with your West African main line—"

"Sorry, wrong," Chester said dryly. "A lot of people jump to that conclusion. But I get my cheekbones and nose from my great-grandmother, who was Cherokee. She disgraced the family on rather a grand scale."

"Oh," Flannagan muttered, clearly disconcerted. "Are you *sure* about that?"

"As sure as I'm ever likely to be." Chester shrugged. "And anyway, it's Mr Freitas's ancestry we're supposed to be discussing, not mine."

Listening, Harold had the horrifying idea that he was going to have to add Chester to the list of people who made him feel inadequate, along with Sparky and Sarah. *It's not fair,* he thought rebelliously. *I'm a long way from stupid even if I don't know as much about history as Sarah does or as much about physics and mathematics as Chester.*

But the twinge passed quickly. He had spent much more time with Chester since the success of the Timescoop project than he ever had before, and he had conceived almost an affection for the cool noncommittal manner of the brown-skinned scientist. In some ways he envied him, for it was already on the cards—so Sparky reported—that he would get a Nobel nomination for his work on the Timescoop within three or four years of the breakthrough's being publicized.

And Flannagan had recovered from his momentary discomfiture and reverted to his normal urbane tones. He was saying, "Well, in accordance with our instructions we examined the verifiable data on the Freitas line and we've isolated nine individuals who had a particularly strong impact on history. It wasn't easy, I may say—seldom have I studied so notable a patrimony! However, here is the final short list, which I trust will meet with your approval."

He handed over a large plastic binder containing nine sheets of parchment-quality paper so stiff it practically crackled to the touch. At the head of each page was a name in bold red Gothic capitals; then followed two or three paragraphs of biographical information in dark green, and at the foot were lists of source material in blue. Harold felt a stir of pride as he read through all of them with close attention.

"The first two Mr Flannagan has selected are people I've already mentioned to you, Chester," he said. "The Sieur Bohun de Freitas was a knight in the service of William the Conqueror and held land from him at a place called Bellisle in Hampshire."

"Subsequently, and regrettably, corrupted to 'Belial' and razed to the ground during the English Civil War by a detachment of Puritans who believed it to be a habitation of the devil," said Flannagan apologetically. "However, I believe some traces of the outer wall and the moat of his castle are still to be seen."

Chester looked doubtful. "It sounds dodgy," he muttered. "Still, I suppose perhaps if there's an old plan of the building, or some exact documentary reference . . . Never mind—carry on."

"The next is Sir Godwin de Freitas-Molyneux, whom I also mentioned to you," Harold said. "His ancestral home apparently does still stand—the one he left when he went crusading."

"That's correct." Flannagan nodded. "A very fine example of a fortified manor house, much improved and added to by later owners but incorporating at least half the original building. That's in northern France, of course—he served the Plantagenet kings of England, who really didn't care too much about that silly little offshore island."

"Then there's someone listed whom I didn't know about," Harold continued. "Reginald de Freitas, Earl of Winchelsea and Poitenne." His tongue rolled with relish around the high-sounding title. "He seems to have been an artistic type—a composer, apparently."

"Precisely," Flannagan said. "While in a sense his impact on history is debatable, he does hold rather a unique position in the development of European culture. According to report, he wrote some outstanding choral music for his private chapel choir, which some authorities maintain was comparable with that of Palestrina half a century later. Unfortunately, none has come down to us, but there's contemporary documentary evidence. And this makes him the forerunner of such notable noble composers as Frederick the Great, who as you presumably know was a skilled flautist and much admired by professional musicians of his day."

Harold stifled a grin. That would be something to impress Sarah, all right! So, too, would the next person on the list. He read aloud, "Edgar Freitas, a courtier of Queen Elizabeth the First, and what's more, a poet, I see."

"A—*minor* poet," Flannagan said apologetically. "But nonetheless a poet, sufficiently distinguished to have found a place in several anthologies of Elizabethan verse. He is also remembered for a scandal involving one of the Queen's ladies-in-waiting and for marrying a distant cousin of Ben Jonson."

Another to impress Sarah with, then. Harold made a mental check mark against the last two names; actually defacing the beautifully printed pages with a hand-held pen would have been a kind of sacrilege.

"It seems to have been at this point that my ancestors crossed the Atlantic," he said, turning to the next entry. "Here's the Reverend Ebenezer Freitas, the one I think I already told you about who has streets named after him in Massachusetts."

Chester nodded.

"Hmm!" A frown crossed Harold's face. "There's less about him here, Mr Flannagan, than about people generations earlier!"

"Yes, I'm afraid so," Flannagan admitted. "It would

appear that at that time people set relatively little store by biography; all the references we can find to him are drawn from church or court records. However, it's plain that he was a major figure in his community, since he not only preached regularly in the church but also held some sort of judicial office, perhaps a magistracy. And, naturally, he does represent the first significant impact of the Freitas family on the New World."

"Whereas Joshua Freitas puts us back in Liverpool, England," Harold noted.

"Precisely. After a period of—well—relative eclipse, the Freitas family suddenly reemerged on the public scene over there with the advent of Joshua, who made a substantial fortune in the West Indian trade, mainly from sugar. His descendants, forming a cadet branch of the family, have included members of Parliament and several mayors, aldermen and other public figures."

"I see." Again Harold made a mental note, this time to track down any of his cousins who were currently holding office in Britain and get them along to the grand reunion celebration. He turned to the next page.

"Ah, we're getting close to home now. I recall my grandfather telling me about Horatio Freitas, who commanded a ship of the line during the War of Independence."

"He later served as a senator, moreover," Flannagan amplified. "A notable public figure in his day."

"And his granddaughter, Tabitha Freitas—she's here, too."

"One could hardly leave her out," Flannagan said with a smile. "She's regarded as one of the North's most valuable secret agents during the Civil War; she gave shelter to scores of soldiers who might otherwise have been captured and shut away in rebel prison camps. She was honored with a reception at the White House after the war, so I'm informed—though, in fact, inspection of White House records has regrettably failed to confirm this. Still, things must have been pretty chaotic at the time; perhaps the entry got overlooked."

"But who's this last one?" Harold demanded as he came to the ninth page. "I never heard of anyone called 'Buffalo Hank'!"

"Ah!" Flannagan looked pleased with himself. "He was a black sheep of your family, Mr Freitas, sorry though I am to have to use such a term. But, of course, standards of judgment change with time, and I felt certain that you'd not be offended if I included him. After all, you no doubt appreciate that such distinguished personages as Daniel Boone were looked down upon, to put it mildly, by polite Eastern society and considered to be illiterate barbarians. But how many people would feel that about Boone nowadays?

"Henry Freitas, who later acquired the nickname of 'Buffalo Hank' by which he's described in my report, was involved in—ah—an irregular liaison with a young lady whose name has not come down to us, and his respectable New England relatives disowned him. So, as many young men of spirit and enterprise did in those days, he went to the western frontier. And since true initiative and vigor cannot be held down, he shortly became a key figure in the opening up of new territories. In particular he was instrumental in helping to establish a line for the Grand Pacific Railroad. Sad to say, he was—as you'll see in my report—eventually killed in a gunfight, but it's virtually beyond doubt that the man who killed him was an outlaw and cattle thief who was himself later *strung up* at Fresno, California, by a vigilante committee. So he got his just deserts in the end."

"Well!" Harold was almost at a loss for words. He got to his feet and held out his hand. "Mr Flannagan, I think you've done me proud. Many thanks indeed for your assistance."

Then, belatedly remembering that Chester was still looking in over the phone, he glanced toward him.

"Have you any questions, Chester?"

"I think I'll save them for the moment," Chester said after a brief pause. "If you could let me have a sight not only of that report but of all the source material it's drawn from, I'll be happy to ponder it for a day or two before making any recommendations."

"I'll arrange that with pleasure, Dr Waley," Flannagan said briskly. "Good day to you both."

When the genealogist had gone, Harold leaned back with a smug smile. This was going to be even better than he'd imagined! To think that among his ancestors he numbered a hero of the Wild West as well as all those prosaic characters who had made fortunes in business or held public office! He almost reached for the phone to start boasting to Sarah about the Elizabethan poet and the noble composer who had been fifty years ahead of his time, but checked the motion before his fingers touched the buttons.

No, it would be best to wait until Chester gave the okay. He didn't completely understand the techniques involved in timescooping something, but he knew it was essential to establish its location to within a few meters at a specified date. It might not be possible to pin down one or more of these notable ancestors sufficiently closely to bring them forward. And he certainly had no intention of permitting a mistake to be made—spending so much power to fetch an anonymous nobody from the past went against his ingrained business instincts.

Still, there it was in good solid print: a summary of his heritage. He stroked the cover of Flannagan's report fondly. Even if they only managed to get hold of half a dozen people of this caliber, they would form an impressive tribute to the Freitas family and create a system-wide sensation. Nobody could possibly discount the importance of the Timescoop technique evolved by a Freitas research project after the massive publicity onslaught which would accompany the family reunion.

And after that . . .

Well, Sarah had mentioned Shakespeare. Why not?

CHAPTER VI

The first time the timid servant girl tried to wake him, Bohun de Freitas burrowed back into the snug, if soiled, pile of pillows and quilts where Ethelfrida was happily snoring away. The second time she was more determined, and he threw a boot at her, but it missed because his eyes were bleary with sleep and bounced off the gray stone wall to land on a hound dozing in the pit it had scrabbled out for itself among the rushes that strewed the floor. The dog's whining complaint sawed into sleep like a clumsy blunt knife, and he cursed forcibly. By the blackness beyond the window—a mere slit in the wall—and the chill which permeated the entire castle it was not yet even dawn. Who in the name of (he caught himself in time and shifted mental gears to avoid invoking one of the Old Gods) Jesus the Christ felt entitled to disturb him at this awful hour?

"My lord," the servant whispered miserably, "there is a courier from the King who waits below. He says King William is on a royal progress through his domains and will be here within the day."

"What?" That fetched Bohun de Freitas out of sleep, all right! Instantly his mind was clear and he was jumping to the icy floor, reaching for his garments discarded last night after much feasting and revelry all anyhow and anywhere.

"Will you come to give him audience, then?" the girl asked.

"In a while. Let him warm himself—make a fire and give him food and drink. But not *good* food and drink, do you understand? Give him stale bread and salt meat and sour wine—or better, sour beer. And listen carefully. Go to the mews and tell Bertrand that he must hide half the falcons; then to the stable and say that the grooms must drive half the horses into hiding in the woods. Then to the kitchens and have the cook conceal half the store of meat in some cool safe place away from the castle. But all discreetly, mind! I have no wish to let this courier suspect what's happening."

A broad grin spread over the servant girl's dull Saxon face. "Yes, my lord!" she exclaimed, and vanished.

Bohun de Freitas chuckled, despite the fact that his fingers were so numb he could barely fasten the thongs of his high leather boots. Ah, he wouldn't have to explain the reason for his orders to these astute retainers of his! Everyone knew that it was fatal to show the King the best of what an estate could provide; it only meant that next time his tax collectors called, the assessment would be so high the winter would be a lean and hungry season beyond necessity.

When he finally tramped down the winding stone stair from the night chamber to receive the royal courier in the great hall, he was almost whistling with satisfaction at his own duplicity.

Sir Godwin de Freitas-Molyneux accepted with pleasure another helping of the rich savory mutton stew that the serving wench poured into his beaten copper dish. His eyes followed her appreciatively as she moved away, waggling her hips. Small wonder these Saracens pictured their paradise as full of houris like her! With her tawny skin and slender limbs she put any of the broad-hipped stolid women of his own country to shame—and who cared that her face was veiled when the rest of her was clad in muslin so light a waft of wind could go through it as through a post-and-rail fence? The face, after all, was far from the most important part of a woman.

Moreover, these silken cushions on which he was reclining were infinitely more grateful to the buttocks than the hard wood or stone of the seats in his northern French manor house. Happily he stuffed the stewed meat past his fringe of moustache with busy fingers and wiped the fingers on his beard as he burped loudly in the approved manner.

Benign, the Saracen leader watched his guest enjoying himself and signaled for more wine to be brought. As a good follower of the Prophet, he himself did not indulge, but it came in handy as a means of befuddling the senses of the infidel.

"It is agreed, then," he purred, "that you will deliver the forces of Duke Raymond into our hands when they approach the walls of Acre?"

"Don't talk to me about Raymond!" Sir Godwin said scornfully. "That greedy, deceitful son of Satan!" He gulped a draught from his newly filled wine goblet and felt mildly surprised at seeing not one but two of the serving wench who had topped it up. "Know what he did? He cheated me out of what was mine by right—I should have been Count of Tripoli if he hadn't gone behind my back to make a deal with that illegitimate double-crosser —what's his name? You know who I mean."

He burped again, far more loudly, and the gas came up his throat accompanied with a sour wave of nausea.

"Ah . . ." He struggled to focus on the Saracen. "Ah . . . Pardon me. I must go out for a second. Your rich food does not entirely—"

He scrambled blindly to his feet and thrust aside the fine silk hangings at the doorway of the tent. With a smirk of satisfaction, his host watched him go. These infidels were all the same—just give them a taste of decent living and they forgot all their vaunted honor in a flash.

"My lord, it is such music as the angels must sing before the throne of the Almighty!" the Bishop of Sandwich declared, crowding like any commoner around the lord of the manor at the exit from his family chapel.

"Praise from your grace is praise indeed," said the Earl of Winchelsea and Poitenne with proper modesty. "For it is well known that few ecclesiastics have a closer knowledge of God's will. If in some humble fashion, I can contrive to give people here and now a foretaste of the bliss to come . . ."

He ended the sentence with a wave of his delicate right hand, much ornamented with gold and jeweled rings, and the Bishop said warmly, "That certainly you do!"

"Oh yes!" chorused the attendant swarm of ladies who had come to hear this latest innovation by the Earl's private choir. Some of them were young and beautiful and, what was more to the point, neglected; their husbands were forever at court about the business of their lord the King, and that was naturally no way to treat a spirited girl not yet turned twenty. The Earl knew that very well—he had had considerable proof of it. And they were not inclined to regard his concern as dishonorable, either, for was it not declared from London to Paris that the Earl of Winchelsea and Poitenne was a godly man whose care was not for the temporal problems of the realm but only for the realm of the hereafter? Why else should he spend so much of his family fortune on maintaining an angelic choir of little boys such as might not otherwise be heard closer to home than Florence or Padua?

As the Bishop withdrew with his train, the ladies took their turn, some touching his hand shyly, some more boldly making open address to him but saying more with their eyes than with their mouths.

When at last he freed himself from the trammels of their admiration, he retreated to his private study and sent for Clarence of Canterbury, who came in as always with a slightly distrait look, his monkish tonsure needing the attention of the razor and miscellaneous blobs of gravy decorating his robe.

"It was well received," said the Earl. "For this I will pay five marks of gold. To what purpose would you desire the money applied?"

"Nothing for myself," Clarence said, looking shocked. But he always said that, and he always ate less and less and he always grew scrawnier and he always wrote more and more beautiful music for the choir, though it likewise became more difficult and there were always more beatings that had to be administered to the choirboys before they got the complex polyphonic lines right. He scratched at his bottom absently as he continued, "Let there be candles set before the shrine of Our Lady of Walsingham, and let there be Masses said for the repose of those who died in sin through no fault of their own, like your ancestor Sir Godwin the Crusader."

"As you wish," said the Earl, privately marking down

the fee from five to two gold coins. Shut away in his own private world of music, Clarence had no faintest notion of the value of money.

Under the gracious old elm trees of Farbingham Hall, Edgar Freitas sat chewing the tip of his quill. Before him on a board there reposed a large plain sheet of white paper; at one corner of the board was a hole into which neatly fitted an inkpot with a chased-silver lid; and within reach on the rustic seat on which he had stopped to rest there was a tankard of ale. The level of the ale had gone down rapidly since he halted. The level of the ink had not gone down at all.

From some distance away he could hear the shrill, hard laughter of Samantha Farbingham playing with her waiting maids at some pointless game of catch-me-who-can. He sighed. It was all right for her, he thought mutinously—at fifteen she was still allowed to have fun and dash around the place in an undignified manner. He, though, trim in his doublet embroidered with gold wire, his hose of plum-colored stuff and his short cloak of brilliant blue, with his sword hanging at his waist and the sun glinting blindingly off the silver buckles of his shoes, was supposed to comport himself like a gentleman and maintain his formality against all odds. Even against summer weather like this, which was more appropriate for setting sail to the Indies than for sitting around biting bits off the end of a quill!

He gathered his determination, dipped the pen in the ink, and laboriously wrote at the head of his sheet of paper: *"Sonnet to the Beloved ——— Composed under Trees at Farbingham Hall."*

Now what name should be bestowed on Samantha for the purposes of the poem? It was unheard of to use a real name in such a context. How about Jemima? How about Margarita? How about—?

He gave up on that subject and started considering the images and conceits he should use. Paps like the buds of a rose? But they weren't—at least none he had ever seen in his eighteen and a half years had borne the least resemblance to a rosebud. They tended to be of a delicate brownish color, whereas roses were always either pure red or bright pink. Hair like gold? But who in the world would want to make love to a girl with stiff metal wires sticking out of her scalp? Let alone the problems which would arise lower down if that were a true comparison!

He took another swig of ale. Then, with decision, he struck through the title he had inscribed on the otherwise blank paper and substituted: *"Ode upon Sir Walter Raleigh's Plantations in the New World."*

Now there was a subject a man could get his teeth into! Only it had one serious drawback: he had never been to the New World and, as things stood, he wasn't going to get the chance. He was going to be hamstrung into staying at the court, and sooner or later pressure from his parents and relatives would inveigle him into marrying some girl of good family like Samantha Farbingham, and he was going to settle down as a staid country squire and raise a mort of children to repeat the process over and over.

Oh, to the devil with poetry for today! He laid aside the board and ink, drained his ale and went off to get some fencing practice with Sir Charles Farbingham's Italian dueling master. Servile and unmanly though he might be, he was certainly the quickest and most agile opponent one could hope to match against.

But to waste one's life on this kind of shadow play was so infuriating, it made him almost wish that Philip of Spain would launch his long-threatened attack on England and put some hint of spice into the world.

CHAPTER VII

By lamplight the Reverend Ebenezer Freitas sat at his table of honest New England wood, knotfree and smooth, shielded from the rattle of rain by snugly fitted shingles and planks. He turned the pages of the Good Book before him, seeking reference after reference that he knew to be relevant without needing to consult the Concordance to tell where the passages he wanted might be found. By the fireplace, his wife, Ellen, sat darning the sleeve of one of the children's coats. The children themselves were upstairs beyond the foursquare beams of the ceiling, having dutifully said their prayers and lain down without complaint. If they had complained—well, there was a good thick leather strap hanging yonder on its peg.

He was just rereading the story of the Witch of En-dor for the dozenth time since the current outbreak of diabolical nuisances, when there came a rap on the outer door. He raised his head and looked as Ellen went to see who was there so late in the evening.

It proved to be Constable Peabody, his cape soaked and glistening from the rain. He came in apologizing for the wetness of his footmarks, removed his hat and stood nervously twisting it round and round in both hands.

"Well?" Reverend Freitas demanded. "Did she confess?"

"Why, yes, sir," Peabody said, and hesitated.

"Well? Why are you not then overjoyed at this triumph of the forces of the Lord?"

"Because, sir—and I hardly know how to say this—she has named as chief among those who attended at the witches' feast where she was given her devil's mark, certain notable personages of the town." Peabody swallowed hard, his Adam's apple bobbing above the wet-shining collar of his cape.

"Who?"

"Why, sir, she named Mistress Coolman first of all."

"And it's not surprising." Reverend Freitas nodded. "She with her giddy ways and her greed to draw men to her! She never did act in the sober, respectable fashion proper to a married woman."

"That's as may be, sir," Peabody said, growing bolder. "But next after Mistress Coolman she named yourself."

There was a stony silence in the room for long seconds. Reverend Freitas could say only one thing in the circumstances, though, and they all knew it. At length he uttered the fatal words.

"Then it was not a true confession, but a wile of the devil to sow dissension among those who hunt down and drive out his black angels. Let her be put to the question in the morning."

Ellen uttered a stifled exclamation. "But, husband dear," she objected—thinking of what the order implied, thinking of the lashings at ankles and neck, thinking of the blood pouring from mouth and nose and near strangulation making the eyes bulge and the little vessels in the white burst until the balls were the color of cherries—"she is barely more than a child! She is only a few months older than our Eliza!"

"Think you I would be less stern with my own daughter were she to give herself to the powers of darkness?" Reverend Freitas thundered. "The question, first thing in the morning! See to it, Constable!"

And he resumed his study of the Good Book.

"Oh, to trouble me with matters of business at this hour is indecent," Joshua Freitas said to his reflection in the mirror. "One needs all one's time to tie a stock in the correct manner, and then lackeys come to distract one with mundane chatter about money and other unimportances. Still, this stock is spoiled—fetch me another," he concluded, and his valet ran to get a fresh one from the pile of three dozen prepared every morning, all stiff with starch and whiter than an unsmutched bank of snow.

A little nervous, for he had never been to Bath before and he was overawed with the atmosphere of gracious living and, above all, with the frenetic gambling he had encountered here, the agent who had traveled down by stagecoach from Liverpool said, "Sir, I was instructed to deliver you the manifests and other papers relevant to your latest venture to the New World—"

"Oh, that!" Joshua Freitas dismissed it with an elegant wave of one slim hand on its way to pick up and sip at his morning cup of chocolate—or rather, his afternoon cup, for midday had chimed from the towers of Bath Abbey twenty minutes before. "All I wish to be told about that is what profit the venture showed. It's devilish hard to make ends meet these days, you know—one can scarcely rub along on less than twenty thousand a year. So just tell me the net figures, there's a good fellow; I have problems of my own to attend to today. That ungentlemanly upstart, Hugh Knightsborough, made some unseemly remarks to my companion at last night's ball, and it would never do for me to call him out in less than the most impeccable attire."

The agent, who was paid forty pounds annually for his services, looked at his employer, looked at the sword hanging in its magnificent enameled scabbard on the back of an empty chair, and swallowed hard. Ah, you had to hand it to these gentry nowadays—they really knew how to live!

Horatio Freitas struggled into his heavy coat of woven metal links disguised with velvet—by himself. It was far safer not to permit anyone else to see him while his vital organs were unprotected. Accordingly, the room was empty and the door was barred. Of course, the stiffness in his right arm from the musket ball he had taken in the shoulderblade during that engagement aboard the *Jolie Marjolaine* made it very awkward to wriggle into the garment, but it was a small price to pay for security.

The velvet, he noticed as he glanced in the mirror, was losing its pile a little at the places where it was most rubbed. It wouldn't do to have some assassin realize that the innocent-seeming coat was actually proof against sword cuts, pistol shot and cudgel blows. It would have to be refurbished shortly—but when would he have the chance to let himself go unprotected for even a day or two so the tailor, sworn to secrecy, could carry out repairs?

Well, no matter. There were constituents of his demanding to see him below, and he needed to wear the coat now lest they prove after all to be British agents bent on the undoing of one of the heroes of the Revolution. His teeth chattered a little as he opened the door a fraction and peered both ways along the landing of his fine house, lined with pictures of his ancestors.

But it would never do for an American gentleman to betray the slightest sign of fear! He clamped his jaws tight together.

About to leave the room, he changed his mind and went back to fetch his pistols from the table beside the bed where they nightly reposed, fully charged with powder and ball. He could carry them into the reception room without exciting much comment, surely; it was logical for a country squire to keep his weapons in good order and he could oil and reprime them as he talked, always having one of the pair ready for use in the event of a surprise attack on him.

Yes, that was a most ingenious idea. He'd have to bear it in mind whenever his constituents called to see him in future.

Tabitha Freitas rolled over lazily in bed and blinked at the sunlight reflected on the ceiling. Something was tickling her cheek—a curious fly, perhaps? She brushed at it and discovered her guess was wrong; it was a frill on the silken nightgown she had discarded some time during the night. Remembering what had caused her to discard it, she turned her head and gazed fondly at the face on the other pillow. So young and innocent he looked in the morning light, even though he was in need of a shave! And to think he had with his own hands shot a man dead only a week before, only a mile or two away!

The idea made her tremble clear through, and she was about to ease herself a little closer and wake the boy up with the nicest possible variety of kiss, when she realized there was a noise outside.

Hurriedly, without disturbing her companion, she pulled on her peignoir—smuggled from Paris by a recent blockade runner—and crept barefoot to the window. As she was peering out to try and see where the cries and rattling of wheels were coming from, the door of the room opened stealthily and Mamma Nell came in.

"You had a good night, missus?" the enormous, very dark old slave said with a throaty chuckle. "I reckoned that row would awaken you, though! It's a general, they say, we can expect next—one from the blue side, though."

"A general!" Tabitha drew herself up. "Goodness me!" What with the wastage of officers caused by this ridiculous war, there had been no lack of majors and colonels in the house, many of them so young one could hardly imagine them bearing the responsibility of such high rank. But a general—that would be a new record.

"But," she added after a second's hesitation, "are you sure he's blue and not gray?"

"Positive, missus," nodded Mamma Nell. "We found a scout from his detachment riding through the west forty half an hour ago."

"Are—are *this one's* men still asleep?"

"Sleeping like exhausted babbies," Mamma Nell assured her. "All strowed about anyhow in the straw of the stables."

"Then don't let them be wakened! And what shall I put on—what's best to receive a general in?" Tabitha hurried to the wardrobe and eased back the door so softly it made no noise to waken the sleeping man. Through her mind was running the impending dialogue:

"General, how wonderful to find you this far south!"

"Not more wonderful, ma'am, than the scheme you worked out to hinder the retreat of the enemy." With a graceful, if rather stiff, bow over her hand. "To find a lady who prizes her country's future above matters of personal honor, that's a marvel indeed. What sacrifices you must have made! What loyalty you must command from your retainers!"

Her daydream rattled happily on.

"How!" said Buffalo Hank Freitas.

"How!" responded Chief Bloody Knife, and there was a companionable pause. During it, the calumet passed three places around the ring.

"You will let the Iron Horse come through your territory," Buffalo Hank said eventually.

"You will give us guns to kill many buffalo," Chief Bloody Knife responded.

There was another silence.

"You will give us firewater," Chief Bloody Knife said.

"I will give you gallons of the best quality firewater."

Then the peace pipe reached him and he had to take the prescribed drag on it, preventing himself from retching only by a violent effort of will. It wasn't just the unsavory yellow teeth of the elderly brave who had sucked at it last; it was also the fact that no one had yet taught these Indians to cure tobacco so that it acquired a decent flavor. But he managed it, and after that there was some friendly gossip which had to be sat through, and finally he was able to get back on his horse and ride to where he had left the U.S. Cavalry detachment in hiding.

"Well?" said the captain in command.

"They're all set up," Buffalo Hank told him. "When they discover that the guns we're giving them are worn-out relics of the Civil War and liable to jam after half a dozen shots, they'll go crazy—especially with the firewater we're shipping in. You did make sure it was well spiked with wood alcohol?"

"Of course."

"Fine. That means the railroad should be free of Indian trouble by the end of the year; they'll just be creeping around the depots in dirty blankets whining for a hand-out. And now, how about my pay for this job, hm?"

CHAPTER VIII

Chester Waley was looking and feeling distinctly unhappy. His depression could scarcely be attributed to the December weather—the Los Angeles climate had reverted to what it had been before the advent of the car, when the clean fuel-cell rendered the old-fashioned gas-burning engine obsolete, and smog was now as much of a memory as the ancient London "pea-souper."

Yet it was as vague as any climatic bringdown. Sitting in his office overlooking the enormous sterile hall where the Timescoop apparatus rested on its dais like a tired spider with supercooled electrum legs, he thought back over the events of the past six months. He recalled the heady elation of the first big success they'd had with the machine he and his colleagues on the project had brought from the stage of barely comprehensible symbols on paper clear through to reliable hardware. He could close his eyes and visualize so acutely it might have been real, the appearance of the statue of Hermes on the receptor platform, its every magnificent curve fresh from the genius sculptor's chisel. Then he had been almost giddy with excitement.

Viewed in the abstract, Harold Freitas's scheme to launch Timescoop on the world by bringing to the present his most outstanding ancestors should also have been an exciting prospect. Granting that the choice of subjects had been made purely to gratify personal vanity, there ought still to have been fantastic enthusiasm in his mind at the idea of talking to people who had been dead for centuries.

And there would be plenty of chances later to bring in the really great men and women of history: Malcolm X was high on his own list, along with Martin Luther King, James Baldwin, Louis Armstrong. The roll call even among his own people was endlessly long.

Yet whenever he sat thinking about it, his mind was numb. He could work up no excitement at all.

Why not? Again and again he had run over the problem in the privacy of his office, lain awake at home far into the small hours, puzzling and pondering. The only reason he could pin down was such a nebulous one that he could barely take it seriously.

He didn't like the genealogist, Flannagan. He found him too smooth, too urbane, too eager to please.

Every instinct cried out for him to go to Freitas directly, beg him to postpone the scheduled date for the big pickup—January first—and reassess all the data on which the plan was founded. But he was sure he could never convince Freitas to do so. There were absolutely no technical problems at all—a dry run had already been carried out on a former member of Freitas Interplanetary's staff, a young man associated with the earliest stages of the Timescoop project who had been killed mountain climbing on a winter vacation and who had proved perfectly amenable to the idea of being brought back to life even though, in order to keep the secret a trifle longer, he had been spirited away to a remote Canadian lodge and was to be kept there until the end of January.

He had come back alive and well, if a trifle frostbitten, and that also should have been a tremendous, uplifting experience. Nonetheless, it had failed to excite Chester Waley.

Precise places and times had been established for all the target subjects: for the Sieur Bohun de Freitas, a day on which it was known from English royal records the King had come to his castle on a progress through his domains; for Sir Godwin de Freitas-Molyneux the day of the battle in which he met his death; and so on down the line. Discreet little teams of three or four close-mouthed experts had been sent to the actual spot in each case, to determine spatial relationships; allowance had been made for continental drift, coastal erosion, subsidence, every other possible cause of error. No, there were no technical arguments he could bring to bear against Freitas's plan. And he was supposed to be purely a technician, a research worker.

Just to top everything off, the inertia of the preparations was probably already too great to be canceled. He leafed through the fat folder of confidential papers that had arrived on his desk that morning. It contained the detailed planning for the family reunion. The news of the reunion itself had already been casually let slip to the media, and present-time relatives had been invited, all expenses paid, to a banquet and ball at the Grand Canyon on January sixth; as yet, however, there had been no inkling that this was anything more than a reunion such as the Schatzenheim clan had held fifteen years before, and indeed it had been presented as a shabby second-best, without even the foundation of something permanent like an automated university to memorialize the event afterwards. Word had come through on the grapevine that Solomon Schatzenheim was being slanderously rude about Harold Freitas in private, calling him an unimaginative copycat and unfit to have inherited the Freitas empire.

Overstamped "SECRET," the later documents in this folder gave the lie to the charge. There were thick memoranda from the department assigned to "acculturate"—Louisa Fold's term—the subjects after their arrival; that would be on New Year's Day itself, following the release to the media of the Timescoop story. During the following five days, the excitement would be allowed to build of its own accord, and then, just prior to the party at the Grand Canyon, there would be a press conference. He was going to have to stand up to fire there himself—he was the man who would have to try and explain the Timescoop technique to the astonished world in words of two syllables or less.

It was not a task he was looking forward to.

Chester nodded his head in reluctant admiration. There was no doubt that his scheme had triggered off something new in Harold Freitas. This job had been planned so thoroughly his eye kept being caught by points he'd never thought of whenever he opened the folder before him. At random, he spotted a report on shoe sizes for the subjects, then a report on those for whom a favorite color had been established; then a linguistic study of Late Norman French; then a table of possible diseases, endemic at the time of origin, which some of them might be carrying. Many of the latter were rather gruesome, and Chester felt himself itching psychosomatically as he reflexively absorbed a passage he hadn't intended to read at all, about the high incidence of body lice in the eighteenth century.

From that point on it became even worse, as a sanitary expert regretfully explained the informal habits of the Middle Ages and suggested intensive conditioning against some of their less savory aspects. Chester slammed the folder shut with a shudder.

Maybe that was his trouble. Maybe he was so much a child of the clean, antiseptic twenty-first century that he couldn't face the idea of people from squalid, insanitary days in the distant past. In which case his antipathy to the project was ridiculous and unjustifiable.

The fact stood: once it got out from under the current load of Freitas's preoccupation with his ancestry, Timescoop was going to be one of the greatest forces for knowledge and understanding of the past ever conceived —probably *the* greatest.

What I need, he told himself, *is to get away from these people who think of it in terms of publicity stunts.*

Not that there was any chance of doing so in the foreseeable future; his current contract had three years to run and it was going to be a long time before Freitas Interplanetary allowed anyone with intimate knowledge of the Timescoop to desert them for another employer, even a noncompetitive employer such as a university.

His phone buzzed, and he reflexively put out a hand to the switch. The screen remained blank and an automatic paging device said, "Dr Waley, is Mr Freitas with you?"

"Ah—no—is he supposed to be?"

"Sorry to have troubled—" the machine began, and another voice broke in: Sarah's.

"That sounds like Chester Waley. Let me talk to him." And in another moment her pretty face, framed today in an electrostatic aureole of her fair hair standing out in a perfect circle, appeared before him.

"Chester, I'd like to ask you a question." She was sitting at a table piled with printed cards; he recognized them as reunion invitations, which—no doubt out of pride—she appeared to be signing by hand instead of passing them through an endorsement machine. She sounded worried.

"By all means," Chester shrugged.

"This—this reunion thing. Do you think it's a good idea?"

Chester hesitated, staring at her. At first, he had had the clear impression that she regarded her husband's plan as nonsensical; within a day or two of its first being broached, however, she had become one of its most enthusiastic proponents, and on the numerous occasions he had been invited to the Freitases', whether for dinner in the LA penthouse or for the two weekends he had spent with them at their country place, she had kept on talking about it with approval. Suddenly for her to have second thoughts was a surprise.

He said noncommittally, "As far as the technical side is concerned—"

"Blast the technical side! I've been signing these invitation cards one after the other until my hand aches, and right in the middle of writing my name for the umpteenth time I stopped and thought: suppose one of these ancestors of Harold's turns out to be an unqualified bastard?"

That's it.

Instantly everything fell into place for Chester, and it became clear why, every time he struggled with the problem, he kept coming back to his own opinion of Flannagan.

"I mean, how much do we really know about these people? One always looks at the past through rose-colored—"

The automatics cut in. "Mrs Freitas! We've found your husband for you and he's ready to take your call."

Sarah scowled. "Oh—very well. But call me back, Chester. I'd like to hear your views. You're the person most intimately connected with the Timescoop project that I've ever spoken to, so I'll be relying on you, remember."

The instant she was off the screen, Chester punched the verbal-interrogation code for Sparky, and the familiar Voltaire mask appeared.

"Yes, Dr Waley?" purred the computer's ingratiating voice.

"Very good," Harold Freitas said in high delight as he passed from room to room in the wing of the Freitas Building which had been set aside for the accommodation of the ultra-distinguished visitors they were expecting during the five days of their acculturation period. The first was done up in gray stone with genuine rushes on the floor, the next to resemble a solar, with natural wooden window seats and a few touches of Saracen luxury such as historians declared a returning Crusader might hanker for, and so on—each a marvel of imaginative reconstruction.

"An emergency call for you, Mr Freitas," said one of the designers who were showing him around. "It's Dr Waley and he says it's very urgent. You'll have to come back out of this section, though—we deliberately didn't install any phones here."

"Damn!" Harold said, but compliantly he traced his steps to the twenty-first century, to find Chester's agitated countenance staring at him from the first phone he reached. His forehead was gleaming with perspiration and his voice quavered.

"Mr Freitas, you've got to cancel the plans for announcing Timescoop! At the very least, you've got to postpone everything while you reconsider your choice of subjects!"

"What?" Harold blinked. "Oh, don't be absurd, Chester! That's absolutely out of the question. Anyway, there's no reason to postpone it. Everything's gone smoothly so far."

"Everything is going to stop going smoothly on January first," Chester said grimly. "I can swear to that."

"Nonsense!" Harold snapped. "Chester, I suspect you've been overworking. Get yourself some tranquilizers, there's a good fellow, and let me finish my tour of inspection here."

He shut off the phone, leaving Chester gloomily contemplating the information Sparky had just dug up for him, which Flannagan had been at such pains to keep concealed.

CHAPTER IX

The impact of the Timescoop announcement, made on January first, 2066, was everything that Louisa Fold and her public-relations department could have hoped for. After the meant-to-be lukewarm response accorded to the boring releases about the Freitas family reunion, which were accompanied by occasional interviews with the far-flung members of the clan designed to suggest that the bottom of the barrel was being scraped—what with these various worthy, but dull local officials and small-town businessmen being singled out—the new data provoked the kind of reaction that might have followed the tossing into a crowd of what everyone assumed to be a harmless firecracker but was in fact a stick of dynamite.

It was as well, in one sense, that automatically self-adjusting programs had been written for Sparky which would enable the Timescoop to pick up the subjects from the past all within the space of a few hours, instead of each single operation of the apparatus being isolated from its neighbor by the need to refocus laboriously on a fresh temporal location. The scientists working on the job wouldn't have been given the chance to concentrate. By noon on the first, every member of the Freitas Interplanetary security corps was frantically chasing intruders through the corridors of the vast building, shunting reporters who hoped for an exclusive to one of the scores of information booths where loop-tape releases were playing over those data which Louisa felt might safely be published at the moment—chiefly romanticized accounts of the careers of the subjects—and simply slinging out the curious and the sensation-seekers after marking their cheeks with ultraviolet ink so that they could be more easily spotted if they tried to sneak in again.

Additionally, every outside circuit was jammed with calls from news media, universities demanding first crack at the technique when it was made commercially available, and religious fanatics in unexpected numbers who wanted to warn Harold Freitas of the impending wrath of God.

By one P.M. they had had to hire a call-filtration service to process them, and Sarah had had to demand a new phone-code from AT & Bell.

Glowing, chewing on a cigar like his grandfather's, Harold leaned back in his deep-padded leather chair and beamed at the faces on the screens before him.

"Marvelous!" he said, and after a pause repeated, "Marvelous! I think we owe your team special congratulations, Chester—it went absolutely without a hitch, didn't it?"

"I keep telling you," Chester muttered. "The hitches are due to start now—or rather, when Helen wakes the subjects up."

"Oh, don't be such a Jonah!" Helen Whymore said. She had been given general oversight of the preparations to receive the subjects, and during the long months of secrecy tension had wound her up to near breaking point. Now, when the cat was finally out of the bag, she was as feverish as Harold. "Everything's working out great. They were all put to sleep, as you know, the moment they arrived in the present, and while they're still unconscious we're checking them over from head to foot. So far"—her eyes flickered to consult another screen in her own office, from where she was speaking—"reports indicate that none of them is carrying any serious contagious disease, although naturally they're all in need of bathing and deodorizing by our standards. Oh!" Her face fell.

"Something wrong, Helen?" Harold jolted forward in his chair.

"Ah—nothing very important," Helen said with forced brightness. "A slight amendment to the reports I just mentioned to you. Apparently Joshua Freitas has—uh—gonorrhea. But I suppose that's only to be expected in the context he comes from."

"Precisely." Harold nodded. "That was a rakehell age, and I understand they didn't have quite our attitude toward such matters." He sounded perfectly matter-of-fact; watching him closely, however, Chester detected that he had been severely shaken by the news.

"And X rays indicate tuberculosis patches on the lungs of the Earl of Winchelsea," Helen continued, still looking at the screen adjacent to her phone. "Apart from that, though, which we can doubtless clear up in a day or two, there's nothing serious wrong with any of them: scabies, body lice, fleas, eczema, impetigo, rheumatism, arthritis, colitis, conjunctivitis, pyorrhea—"

She checked herself suddenly, aware belatedly of the length of the list she was reading out. "Well, as I say," she concluded, "nothing we can't cope with in a matter of hours or, at most, of days."

"Hmm!" Harold pressed his lips together; it seemed to Chester that, in spite of the careful analysis of the problem made by the medical historians the company had retained, this was the first moment he had actually believed that his ancestors might be heirs to the ills of the flesh which were so prevalent in less civilized times. However, he maintained his self-control admirably. "That's very reassuring, what Helen has told us—isn't it?" He half-scowled until he had had a series of dutiful nods from all the screens except the one connected to Sparky, even Chester having to admit that he was expecting something infinitely worse. One case of VD and some common skin, eye and mouth infections seemed like getting off lightly.

"Now when they're medically passed fit," Harold resumed, "we wake them up—or rather let them wake up in environments which won't shock them. Of course, they'll realize they're not in their own homes, or wherever they started from; in particular, Sir Godwin has been —ah—collected from a battlefield in Palestine and is probably more used to tents than the sort of room we've assigned to him. At least, though, it won't be wholly foreign to his experience. From then on we start a program of adjustment, planned to compress the salient facts about their arrival in 2066 into at most three days, and couched in terms historians assure us ought to be comprehensible to them. The closer they come to our own day, naturally, the fewer problems of communication we expect to run into. We have accelerated language tuition available for those who don't speak a recognizable variant of modern

English; we have proper clothing available which fits them and will be comfortable in their terms. And so on. It all seems to be well under control. So let's turn to your department, Louisa. How has the public's response been so far?"

"I've got a call-filtering service monitoring the literally thousands of calls we've taken today," Louisa said and, like Helen, turned to look at a data-screen out of the field of her phone-camera. "So far they break down into the following major categories: a sudden flood of demands to be invited to the Grand Canyon party, including a feeler from the White House which I earmarked for your personal attention; large numbers of calls from historians and other academics insisting that we must make available to them various historical personages, including Tiglath-pileser, Benedict Arnold, Chief Crazy Horse, Nell Gwyn and Messalina—the last two, by the way, from the Institute of Sex Research at Indiana."

"Are they still operating?" Harold said, marveling. "Well, well! Sorry, go on."

"And the only remaining category of any size is composed of calls from people who are apparently afraid that we're going to bring back Jesus, Mohammed and the Buddha."

"So we are," Harold said comfortably. "So we are. In fact, according to the last check I made with Sparky, it's a toss-up whether we should bring back first of the general subjects Jesus, Napoleon or George Washington."

"At present," the computer said, "it's George Washington by five points. This would appear to be an index of public confidence in the candidates' relative ability to stand up to their respective contemporary images."

"Very probably," Harold said, but Chester felt that his real area of interest didn't lie in those later questions; he was far more concerned with his own family. "But in general, Louisa: are we getting the response we hoped for?"

"And how!" Louisa said smugly.

"In that case, I think we can conclude this conference. Oh! One thing before I dismiss the meeting: you are, of course, all cordially invited to the actual reunion party on the sixth. I don't know whether I remembered to mention that before."

Grinning like a well-fed cat, he cut the circuit.

"As a matter of fact, you didn't," Chester murmured as the screen blanked.

"Didn't what?" said a voice from behind him, and he spun his chair. Unnoticed, Sarah had crept into the office and was standing within arm's reach, but out of the line of the phone-camera.

"Sorry! I didn't hear you come in," Chester said, scrambling to his feet. "Can I do anything for—?"

"What was it Harold didn't do?" Sarah insisted.

"Ah—remember to invite us to the Grand Canyon party until a moment ago."

"That sounds typical of Harold." Sarah sighed, moving to a chair. She was looking especially beautiful today, in a nearly transparent knee-length chiton-style gown of white shot through with pale lime-green. "Sometimes I get the impression that he really believes he brought all this about by himself."

"That's okay provided he's willing to take the blame himself as well," Chester said. He hadn't meant to speak so bluntly, but the words were out before he could check them.

Sarah stared at him. "That's right—I forgot. You were going to call me back and let me know your honest opinion of this crazy scheme, and you never did. It's a bit late now, of course, but tell me, anyway."

Chester hesitated. He said after a pause, "What brings you down here, if I might ask that first?"

"What do you think? I exercised the privileges of rank—not to mention the privileges of having married into the Freitas family—and came down to take a look at the—"

"Subjects?"

"What a word! But that's how they're being treated, come to think of it: just lying there unconscious while all kinds of scientists poke and probe at them. I thought it would be a terrific thrill to see people from the past for the first time; instead, what I saw could just as well have been stone dead for good and all. Though—"

"Yes?"

"Though I must say I was struck by one or two things. How small the ones are from furthest back—barely up to my shoulder." She chuckled. "And Edgar, the one from the court of Queen Elizabeth the First who wrote all that superficial but elegant poetry: he does look like a doll in spite of his silly half-grown beard."

She briskened. "Stop prevaricating, though, Chester. I know you well enough by now to recognize when you're trying to dodge the issue."

Reluctantly Chester said, "Well—ah—did it ever strike you that a genealogist like Flannagan can—how shall I put it?—can pander to the vanity of his clients and hide behind his status as an expert at the same time?"

The half-smile which had lit Sarah's face as she thought of Edgar Freitas vanished. She said, "Oh my God. Do you mean Harold has been conned again?"

"All I can do is show you these printouts from Sparky," Chester shrugged. "It looks as though, in all the months we've spent preparing for the big day, nobody but me thought of putting these particular questions, and I—being a shortsighted idiot—only thought of doing so after you called me the other day, when it was far too late to stop the project. Here!"

Violently he thrust at her the fat stack of documents the computer had delivered to his office, and she turned them over one by one. Her face grew paler with each page, and at intervals she whispered, "Oh, my God. Oh, my God."

CHAPTER X

"The bastard," Solomon Schatzenheim said, pacing up and down the living area of his Long Island home. It being New Year's he had learned the news at home instead of his office, where he would normally have found it among a digest of the day's events routinely prepared for delivery to his desk. He said again, "The *bastard!*"

"Who?" Miriam inquired, turning her sleek dark head away from the three-vee screen on which she was watching a news bulletin that so far had been entirely devoted to the Freitas reunion.

"Harold Freitas, of course! He must have fooled me and everyone else! Nobody outside the company seems to have had an inkling of what was going to happen, and a hell of a lot of people inside didn't get wind of it, either. Which reminds me: I must cut off our retainer to that useless agent of ours—what's his name? Detrick, that's the one. Sold us a computer-interrogation code for Sparky and never gave us a hint of this time-retrieval process! Nobody knew *anything!*"

"*I* knew," Miriam said calmly.

"What?" Solomon stopped dead in the middle of the floor and his face went the color of a turkey-cock's wattles.

"I knew," Miriam repeated. "I've become pretty good friends with Sarah Freitas over the past six months, and I knew she was bursting with some kind of secret. So about eight or nine weeks ago I got her to let me in on it. It took quite a bit of prying, but in the end she opened up."

"Why in the name of all that's holy didn't you tell me, then?" Solomon roared.

"I thought you deserved not to be told," Miriam said. "I simply felt sick of the way you shut me out of your life except when you need me to act as hostess for a party or something. Speaking of parties reminds me: I asked Sarah to make sure we were invited to this family reunion at

Grand Canyon. I must start thinking about what I'm going to wear."

"You go to that party over my dead body!" Solomon stormed forward and seized her by the wrist, yanking her to her feet.

"That would be a pleasure," Miriam sighed. "But in fact it's too much to hope for, isn't it?"

"No, Mr Freitas," Quentin, the head of research, said firmly. "We dare not jeopardize the success of this project by letting you in to see or talk to the subjects now they've been awakened. Four or five days is a short enough time in all conscience to make them understand what's happened to them, so we absolutely must ensure that the series of inevitable shocks they'll have to cope with is properly graduated. By far the most violent shock of all will be to confront a stranger of their own age—or considerably older, in the case of young Edgar—and have to accept that this is their umpteenth great-grandson. The morning of the reunion party is the earliest, as well as the latest, possible moment we can permit you a face-to-face introduction. In the interim, we shall have to take advantage of every single moment we have to indoctrinate them, calm their minds, evaluate and analyze their behaviour. I'm sorry, sir, but that's Sparky's own opinion and I'm sure you wouldn't question his judgment."

"No, I suppose not," Harold said grumpily. Nonetheless, the so-short five days between scooping up his ancestors and the first chance he was going to get to talk to them—with the implied corollary that they would thank him for giving them the unique opportunity to see the world of the future—were stretching into an interminable eon, and, gratifying though they were, such punctuation marks as the several-times-daily calls from three-vee asking him to make a guest appearance and the never-ending flood of favorable sales and advertising figures were doing nothing to free him from his fever of impatience.

He dismissed Quentin with a wave and went back to his guest list for the party on the sixth. One name had been added to it this morning which gave him genuine pleasure, and it wasn't the President's.

It was Solomon Schatzenheim's. He was planning to come along with his wife, Miriam.

Yet it wasn't enough merely to read the note of acceptance. He wanted to see Solomon right there before him, watch him turn green with envy as the choir of Our Lady Queen of the Angels, specially retained for the occasion, gave the first performance in centuries of a motet by the Earl of Winchelsea, while the poet Edgar recited his own sonnets, while . . .

He drifted away on a tide of rose-colored daydreams.

"Now look!" Cy Detrick said desperately to the phone over which the anonymous call had just come. There was a scrambler in the circuit so that only the sound was reaching him, and that was distorted. The screen was a polychrome swirl, like a rainbow that had been through an electric blender.

"I told you, your retainer has been discontinued and there's no question of arguing," the stranger from Four-S emphasized.

"Yes, I know I fell down on this family-reunion thing!" Detrick whimpered. "But—but look! How's about if I get you some dirt on these ancestors, the kind of dirt you could use?" The inspiration had that second come to him; he had no idea where he was going to get the goods from, but it seemed like a fair bet. Who, after all, had a perfectly clean record?

"What kind of dirt?" said the caller after a moment of hesitation. Detrick gained the clear impression that the pause had been to consult someone who was sitting in on the conversation, perhaps even Solomon Schatzenheim himself.

"Well—uh—" Detrick's mind raced, then faltered. These days, what would have made a good blackmail lever a century before was taken for granted by the public; no one gave a hoot for sexual kinks or conventional veniality. He grabbed at a straw floating by in the torrent of his thoughts.

"Well, there's someone I can put some pressure on.

Someone I didn't realize had been retained by Freitas for any particular reason. He's a genealogist. I never knew one of those who didn't pretty up the family trees of his clients, did you? I bet I can dig a lot of good dirt out of him."

There was another interval of silence. Finally the caller said, "Very well. Go ahead. You have seventy-two hours."

"Wait a second! Ah—it could be expensive. I mean, if he's the kind of expert Freitas would hire, he must be at the top of his class . . ." The words trailed away.

With obvious contempt, the caller said, "You mean you want something to bribe him with. No. If he's as successful as you say, he can probably get enough in fees to make him immune. You just talk to him, you just butter him up a bit. And remember: from now on you're being paid by results, or not at all."

The screen blanked and left Detrick chewing his lower lip so hard he eventually noticed the taste of blood under his tongue.

"It didn't work," Miriam said to the phone. She was almost on the verge of tears. "And I'd been banking on it—I was *sure* it would make him angry enough to hit me so I could sue him for divorce! All it's done is make him look like a fool, and that means he'll be worse than ever to live with."

"He's not the only one," Sarah said. She also was very pale, though controlling her emotions better. "Harold is going to look like worse than a fool."

"But how can that be?" Miriam demanded. "He's brought it off perfectly so far—everyone's sick with envy and the status of Freitas Interplanetary has gone rocketing up in the past couple of days!"

Strained, Sarah told her.

"The only consolation is," she concluded, "there's one man involved in the project with his head screwed on right: Chester Waley. He's not actually supposed to be anything except a scientist, but he does think about things before he starts on them, and he's promised to do his uttermost to prevent any trouble on the sixth. I hope to goodness he and Sparky between them can come up with something. When I think of everyone who's going to be there—

the President, Solomon, all those relatives we've gone to so much trouble to dig out from God knows where—I practically faint with terror!"

"How am I going to tell Mr Freitas?" Louisa said to Helen Whymore.

"Yes, of course, Mr Detrick," Flannagan said. "One does—ah—*weight* one's findings a little to present the client's ancestry in the most favorable light. It's no secret; it's mere humanitarianism."

He reached for his computer board, chuckling. "However, it's a harmless failing—vanity. We all suffer from it a little, don't we? Now, about your own family tree . . ."

"How are we going to tell Freitas?" mourned Helen Whymore to Sparky in the privacy of her office.

The only possible conclusion seemed to be that he'd have to find out for himself. Even Sparky couldn't offer a better alternative.

"Haven't you told Harold?" Miriam demanded.

"I thought about that," Sarah said. "But then I talked to Chester Waley again, and he said he'd tried to warn Harold before it was too late, and Harold simply refused to listen. So I think it might be a salutary shock for him. I'm just going to let things ride as they are and make sure I'm standing well back when it comes to the inevitable crunch."

Miriam shivered. "I'm not sure I'm looking forward to your party on the sixth," she admitted. "Not now."

That made her one among several of the intending guests, all the rest of whom were actually engaged on the project.

CHAPTER XI

Harold Freitas had contrived to prevent himself from paying attention to the gathering air of gloom in the Freitas Building, even though every time he spoke to people involved with the Timescoop project, it showed on their faces. But he dared not let himself wonder about its cause. Too much was hanging on the success of the reunion party that night. Every news service on the planet was going to cover it, and even the struggling independent services from Mars and the moons of Jupiter, which almost never bothered to send a reporter to Earth, had asked for press admission cards. The President was definitely going to be there, and right that minute Secret Service agents were checking out the security precautions at the Grand Canyon site.

Accordingly, he marched into the wing of the building where his ancestors had been medically treated, if necessary taught modern colloquial English, and gradually adjusted to the idea that they were centuries or even a millennium ahead of their own age; held out his hand to shake with Helen, Louisa and James Quentin; and beamed around at the various junior staff attending them. He recognized Chester hovering in the background, but apart from him he could not have recalled the names of any of the others. Not to worry—names had never been his strong point.

"Well!" he exclaimed, beckoning for Sarah to come and stand at his side. "You've kept us on tenterhooks long enough—and I must say it was a new experience for me, being kept away from part of my own company's headquarters! But that's all over, and this is a great day, isn't it? A day that will go down in history!"

"Well . . ." Helen swallowed hard. "Yes, Mr Freitas.

But perhaps not for the reasons you're expecting. We've done our absolute utmost, but—uh—we didn't really have as much time as it proved we should have had."

A chilly sensation began to gather in the pit of Harold's stomach. He said faintly, "I don't think I quite—"

"Well, you damned well should!" Sarah snapped. "Chester tried to tell you over and over. You didn't listen."

Keeping well in the background, Chester winced and turned away, muttering something that his nearest neighbors later guessed might have been: "Don't you lay the blame on me!"

"This way," Helen said determinedly, and led the party toward the room where the Sieur Bohun de Freitas had been installed.

When he heard the knock on his door, Bohun de Freitas started. He had been staring at the three-vee screen his extraordinary keepers had brought in the day before yesterday, which kept presenting him with barely comprehensible mobile images sealed off behind a glass screen. He had seen two or three comely wenches in incredibly immodest garb, but not all his ingenuity had contrived to bring them forth from the box and enable him to enjoy them. What else was a man supposed to do to pass the time when he was mewed up like any falcon, without even the falcon's blessed gift of being able to forget the world when the hood dropped over its eyes?

They had talked about books—but what business did a grown man have with books, unless he was a priest? That was why the soft English had caved in before the onslaught of King William's forces: too much book learning had made them forget the martial arts, copying their own King Alfred, who, for all they claimed he had built them a navy, had spent his days in poring over dusty parchments. A king who could not merely read, but even write—it was ridiculous!

As he rose, he found himself face to face with a man of decent tallness, indeed of much greater height than himself, but of slack muscle and with a potbelly that almost invited a jesting jab with a sword. He restrained the impulse. Doing his best to attune his ear to the harsh, barbaric sounds of this strange new tongue, he listened with what patience he could muster to the introduction the woman called Helen was performing. That, of course, was another thing that had gone wrong with the world since his day—if it were true that he had indeed been snatched a thousand years across time, which he still found questionable. What were women doing in positions of influence? Above all, what were they doing among his captors? No matter that they dressed more like men than the men did, with their short gowns and their hose of strange new stuffs—they were still women, soft-faced and beardless, and it was a crying indignity for a landed lord who had raped a score of better-favored wenches in his travels to have to hold his tongue meekly and obey their orders!

"This is your distant grandson, Mon Sieur," said the woman Helen. "Harold Freitas, third of that name! It is thanks to him that you are here now, having been fetched across time—"

"Did you say *Harold* Freitas?" echoed Bohun.

"Why—" Alarmed, Helen took a step back. "Why, yes!"

"And he claims to be a descendant of mine?"

"Y-yes!"

"You lie! You lie in your teeth!" Bohun, blind with fury, looked around for a weapon, but in this decadent age there were no swords or axes in this room where he had been penned up. Never mind! So soft and weak a traitor could be torn apart with the bare hands!

He snarled and launched himself at the one allegedly called Harold, and the world went blank.

"I'm sorry we had to tranquilize him like that, Mr Freitas," Helen whispered as they closed and locked the door behind them. She was still trembling from the shock. "But—uh—well—"

"It's perfectly clear what made him so annoyed," Sarah said. "As far as he's concerned, Harold is the name of the English traitor king who tried to welsh on the oath he'd made to William of Normandy when he promised to acknowledge him as his overlord if he'd help him secure the English throne. That was what the Norman invasion was all about, you see. How would you like it if you found out that one of your descendants had been baptized Benedict Arnold Freitas?"

"But he practically tried to kill me!" Harold exploded. "If someone hadn't been quick with that tranquilizer gun, he'd—he'd have torn me limb from limb!"

"Why should you be so surprised?" Sarah countered. "He's a Norman, isn't he? And 'Norman' is the same word as 'Norseman' originally. He went berserk, just as you'd expect him to."

"But . . ." Harold's objection trailed into silence. "Are we likely to have the same trouble with the rest of them?" he asked at length.

"Oh, no, I can assure you of that," Helen Whymore said. "But each of them does present a problem of his own. Here, this is where we've lodged the crusader, Sir Godwin."

Sir Godwin smiled as the knock came at his door and the visitors entered. There had certainly been progress in the centuries that had supposedly passed since his day—he had been luxuriating in the comfort of the cushions spread around his room. How that old Saracen devil Ibn-addin would have envied them! And the food he had been given, and the wines! He shook his head, marveling. There was only one drawback he had yet been able to detect in this strange new world, and that was to date a trifling one. Doubtless with the passage of time it would be solved. This distant age was full of fine buxom young women, dressed in a style calculated to inflame any normal man, and so far he had been denied company on his nightcouch. Still, he knew he was a handsome man, and after the attentions of the bathman and the various perfumes and ointments he had requested and been given, he was even more presentable than ordinarily. The tips of his beard were practically dripping with the aromatic grease they had found for him, similar to but not the same as spikenard. Never in all his days could Ibn-addin have cut a greater dash!

With many flourishes and extravagant declarations of his indebtedness, he made the visitors welcome; in particular he embraced his far-distant descendant who had brought him back to life—strange though the idea still was. Having seated them, ordered coffee and wine and sweetmeats, he broached a subject which had been close to his heart since first he learned a little about the present day.

"Tell me," he murmured, "is it true that there are still followers of the prophet Mohammed in this world of yours?"

Trying not to fidget as the grease from Sir Godwin's disgustingly sticky beard trickled down his cheek, leaving a track of itching like a louse, Harold said, "Why, yes, there are."

At least this one hadn't tried to murder him on sight!

"And are they—shall we say?—better provided with the luxuries of life than the Christian portion of mankind?"

"Oh, no." Harold shrugged. "We in the West enjoy the highest standard of living in the whole of history."

"Ah! It is as I suspected. The devotees of the true God have finally got the better of those lying spawn of Satan who so often beguiled me with fair words and then betrayed me, knowing nothing of knightly honor." Sir Godwin sipped the coffee that had been set before him; it was unlike anything he had been accustomed to in his former existence, but it was extremely good.

"Tell me something further, then," he went on, wiping his shaggy moustache with the back of his hand and giving an appreciative burp. "Have you not in this world weapons of war such that they could wipe out whole cities in a blink of the eye? I think they are called 'bombs' and are in some fashion projected through the air by pyrotechnical devices."

"He asked for a military manual to be piped to his three-vee screen directly he understood the principle of it," Helen whispered to Harold. "And of course, since he was a notable warrior in his day, we couldn't very well refuse."

Harold nodded and cleared his throat. "That's so," he agreed.

"And also means to burn up the enemy, at a distance, over miles, with the device they call a 'laser'? And means to sow pestilence secretly in water and food, so subtly that no man could know from whence it came?"

"Well . . ." Harold hesitated, but the admission was forced from him. "Actually we do have all these things."

Sir Godwin leaned forward confidentially and placed on Harold's knee a hand dripping with coffee he had spilled and greasy from touching his beard so thick with ointment. "And are you not a man of great wealth and power?"

"I think I can safely lay claim to that," Harold said, looking modestly at the floor and trying not to think of what Sir Godwin's touch was doing to his best pair of formal shorts.

"Then my plan can be realized!" Sir Godwin leaped to his feet, overturning his coffee cup and a wine jug he had set down too close to the hem of the swinging surcoat. "You and I between us shall finish the work begun by those overfrail vessels of the true faith, Raymond and Bohemond and Robert of Normandy! This very day we shall set about assembling such weapons of war as may destroy the infidel for ever, and we shall be the most honored of men! The name of Freitas shall stand until Judgment Day as a monument to the victory of the Christian knights!"

It took the party some time to extricate themselves from the eager crusader's company, but at last they were back in the corridor and Harold was mopping at the various smears his ancestor had left on his skin and his clothing.

"Heaven preserve us," he muttered. "Is that all he can think of?"

"He's changed his tune," Sarah said. "According to what Sparky dug up for us, he was killed by one of his own side because he'd sold his companions out to the Saracens."

"Never!" Harold dropped his handkerchief in his agitation.

"That's right," Chester confirmed, looking gloomy. "He was angry with Duke Raymond because he thought he'd been cheated out of the county of Tripoli. What else do you expect someone like that to think of except exterminating the infidel when he's told about hydrogen bombs and rocket missiles for the first time?"

Harold had gone as white as paper. Gathering his forces with an effort, he said, "Well, at least the next on the list won't be such a bloodthirsty type, will he? The Earl of Winchelsea is the one who's remembered for his music, and that's an innocent enough pastime."

"Ah . . ." Not for the first time, Helen seemed to have difficulty finding words. "We have some reservations about him, too."

"Oh, Jesus," Harold said. He let his hands fall to his sides and stood up like a man facing a firing squad. "Such as what?"

"Well, we did as we were instructed and we hired the choir of Our Lady Queen of the Angels and brought them along for him to coach in this item he's supposed to perform at the party tonight. We'd already given him the most authentic reconstructions of the instruments of his day that we could lay our hands on—shawms, rebecs, rackets, the lot, in the hope that he'd at least be able to get a tune out of one of them. He tossed them in a corner and he hasn't touched them since. So then when we told him what we wanted, he said he would have to teach the boys their parts individually, one at a time, which seemed reasonable because musical notation in those days bore practically no resemblance to the modern version. But—" Helen spread her hands. "The kind of thing he seemed to want to instruct these nice young boys in bore no resemblance to music of any kind, and we've had to pay quite a lot of hush money to the parents of the two who came out screaming because of what he tried to make them do."

"So that's why I got such a large requisition from the legal department this week!" From the rear of the group, Louisa thrust her way forward, paling. "You mean he's a phoney—not a composer at all but a dirty old man?"

"As far as Sparky can make out," Sarah said loudly and clearly, "he never learned anything about music. He just picked the brains of some poor anonymous monk whose work he passed off as his own. Shall we skip him and go on?"

CHAPTER XII

The universe seemed to be tumbling around Harold now, spinning insanely like a badly topped billiard ball. He never knew how he managed to locate his voice among the wild confusion of these successive shocks, but he did, and heard words come croaking out.

"Why didn't anyone tell me about these difficulties?"

"Several people tried to," Sarah answered unsympathetically. "You simply didn't listen."

"But aren't any of these ancestors of mine what I was told they were? Are they all lunatics or fakes?"

"Oh, one or two of them are perfectly presentable," Helen Whymore soothed. "We're just coming to Edgar, for instance, and he's very nice indeed—in fact, he's charming."

"Yes, he's an absolute dear," Sarah agreed, and Harold shot a suspicious glance at her.

"How do you know he's a dear?"

But all she gave him by way of answer was an enigmatic smile. He hesitated a second over whether to pursue the matter and decided against it.

"Very well, then." He sighed. "Let's hope we've got at least one salvageable ancestor out of this gang of cheats."

No voyage to the Indies could compare with this fantastic trip into time! Edgar Freitas had been half beside himself for days on end, ever since they first informed him what had happened. They'd taken long enough over the explanations in all conscience, as though they expected him to be frightened. How, though, could someone be frightened who had lived through such wonderful changes in the world as Gloriana's star had shed its benignant rays upon? Gone were the ancient silly tales of men with their heads in the midst of their bodies, of the Anthropophagi and the Upas tree; in their place, authentic stories retailed by honest travelers, who carried marvelous new discoveries in their baggage to shore up their claims—potatoes, tomatoes, human scalps dried in the sun and kept as trophies by the savages of the New World, and clay pipes designed to drink the smoke of that intoxicating brown leaf *tabaco* through.

If only they would let him out to savor the wonders of this world himself.

But he had at least a window, a sort of magic window he could peer through. This thing they called a "VVV-set"—no, correction: a "three-vee set"—it was such a marvel as Master Shakespeare's witches in the play of *Macbeth* could not have conjured forth to display their lying promises upon!

A tap at the door, and in came the inhabitants of this incredible new day: chief among them a man he had not yet been presented to, stately in bearing with something of the elder Lord Cecil's presence for all that he seemed shy and yet clearly could not be, for he was the one—so his companions said—whose wealth and wisdom had fathered forth such a miracle. With him, too, was the beauteous lady, though somewhat overtall, who had stolen into his room a day gone by and spoken knowledgeably with him of the poet's art, and of madrigals, and of another far sweeter subject not to be mentioned among strangers, and left enjoining him to silence; and—wonder of wonders—a man with skin browner than seasoned oak, perhaps one of the veritable Indians that (had he understood aright where on the round globe he was) abounded on this, the continent across the ocean from his home.

"Ah, sir!" he declared to the person who claimed to be his own distant grandson (and yet it was impossible to make himself feel that in his bones, he who for all his eighteen years and a half had fathered no children and had little more than snatched amours in a garret or a thicket to brand him a man among men). "I shall write such an ode to your honor! I shall build conceits more than any man yet trapped in the web of verse! I shall bleed over my poems, I shall weep over them and still not have reflected half the honor due to you!"

Why, he wondered in a distant corner of his mind, *did the lovely lady standing close by the door smile at his promises?*

"Well, that's a relief," Harold said as they took their leave of Edgar Freitas. "He does seem like a nice young chap, and not in the least disturbed by what's happened to him."

"He has good reason, Sparky says," Chester countered in a sour voice. "Just about the time we managed to locate him, he got bored enough to seduce the mother of a girl he was supposed to be interested in, one of Queen Elizabeth's maids of the bedchamber, and he's probably delighted that he didn't have to stay and face the consequences. At least, not in this version of himself."

"Ah . . ." Harold struggled manfully with his own reactions, and won—for the moment, at least. "He's a good-looking boy, of course, and I'm sure she was flattered by his attentions."

"Quite right," Sarah said cheerfully. "Who's next—Ebenezer, isn't it?"

Quentin, Helen and Louisa looked uniformly doleful. They exchanged glances as though wondering who should take on the unpleasant duty of speaking up. In the end none of them did; they merely moved to the next room and opened the door.

"Get thee behind me, Satan!" roared Ebenezer Freitas as the door opened. With fingernails and teeth and God-given patience, he had contrived to make himself a kind of crucifix out of strips of wood and threads teased from the hem of the horrible devilish garments he had been given to put on. They were at least moderately decent, he had to grant, compared to the garb affected by the devil's servants who had come into his prison to try and tempt him. Bare legs to the knee and higher! Bosoms disgustingly outlined under fabric flimsier than butter muslin! And the men were as bad!

No: *not* men. Imps of Satan. That was what they must be. Their lies about bringing him into the future—what a transparent device! This must be hell, for all that it was comfortable, warm, fresh-scented. He must have been singled out for special trials, like the saints of old, an honor which bid fair to induce in him the fatal sin of pride against which he had been struggling night and day since he realized what the Evil One had done to him.

This time, at least, he won without a struggle. Seeing him charge at them with crucifix upraised, the intruders beat a hasty retreat.

"Not another one who wants to kill me!" Harold moaned.

"Not exactly, Mr. Freitas." Helen wiped a trace of perspiration from her broad white forehead. "As nearly as we can figure it out—because since his awakening he has absolutely refused to talk to us directly—he thinks that this is all a device of the devil to tempt him into forsaking Christianity."

"Then he must be mad!"

"Not by his own lights," Sarah said. "Don't you know what made your distinguished ancestor distinguished? Sparky told us. He was among the most enthusiastic hunters-down of witches in the days of the Salem trials, a man who swallowed every crumb of fabricated evidence that any lying teenage girl tossed his way, who eventually supervised the torturing of his own wife and daughter to secure confessions from them."

"It's a lie!" Harold whispered.

"Go punch for Sparky," Chester snapped, and turned away. He was regretting that he had to witness this miserable farce—yet he still could not see that there was any point at which he could have prevented it.

"Well, we can't produce him for—for public inspection," Harold groaned. "Haven't you found me anyone sane and reasonable except the Elizabethan fellow? He seems decent enough, and I suppose even by himself—but the news releases promised all nine of them would be at the party!" He glared at Louisa Fold.

"Don't please start telling me that I've let you down!" she snapped. "It's not my fault if these much-vaunted ancestors of yours prove on close examination to be nut cases or—" She broke off, putting her hand to her mouth. "Goodness, I'm sorry!" she exclaimed. "I didn't mean to say anything like that. I—I must be awfully tired, I guess."

But Harold's exact turn of phrase was ringing back and

forth in Chester's memory: "Haven't *you* found me anyone . . . ?" Apparently he was getting ready to convince himself that this, along with everything else that had happened since he was forced into the presidential chair of Freitas Interplanetary ahead of schedule, was actually to be blamed on other people.

And if he managed to pull that trick off, Chester promised himself, he was quitting, contract or no contract.

"Well, Joshua Freitas is quite a civilized character," Helen said, with the air of someone putting an overdue finger in a breached dike of good manners. "Shall we drop in on him? You've seen his accommodation, but some people haven't, and I think it's particularly successful, far more so than the Norman castle at the beginning or even the Elizabethan quarters in which we installed Edgar."

"Don't make a sound," Joshua Freitas enjoined as the door opened. *"Shhh!"*

Standing compliantly in the doorway and looking around at the décor, which was rampant Chinoiserie based largely on the Brighton Pavilion, a riot of red and gilt dragons, Harold waited. When the silence had dragged on longer than he could stand, he said, "Er—forgive me, but what are you doing that needs such concentration?"

"Spoiled it!" Joshua leaped to his feet. "Sir, a man must find what pastimes he can in a dreary environment like this in which you've penned me, as though I were a debtor cast into Newgate Jail. Across this tabletop—"

"But you have a three-vee set, and surely that—"

"Sir, one gentleman permits another to complete his speech before commencing his own," Joshua said sternly. "As I was saying: across the top of this table"—he tapped it; it was rather a handsome piece, of lacquer and bamboo—"I have been racing two lice one against the other, betting on which will cross this painted flower-stem first."

"Lice!" Harold said in horror. "Lice!"

"Have you never heard it said that it is an ungenerous brain that breeds no lice?" Joshua responded.

Harold glanced wildly from one to other of his companions. Helen shrugged. "He seems to believe that, so we had to—uh—give him a few of them back after we'd cleansed him."

"Well, he can't bring any of those to the party tonight. That's definite!" Harold was shaking with repressed nausea. "And has he no other interest except gambling?"

"Fighting," Chester said sourly. He pointed at the sword propped alongside Joshua's louse-racing table.

"I'm afraid that's so," Quentin confirmed. "He wanted to challenge me to a duel yesterday, and when I said we didn't do that kind of thing any longer, he used the most abusive language—which, of course, I turned a deaf ear to. That merely seemed to confirm his opinion of me."

"But surely someone from Beau Nash's day at Bath would know how to comport himself at a party," Harold said. "I mean, I get the idea that they did practically nothing else. Except for gambling, naturally. And he's rather an impressive sight in that outfit of his, with the powdered wig and so on."

"I think he's rather handsome," Sarah said. "But I imagine he's an incredible bore."

"Bore or not," Harold said with decision, totally ignoring the implied insult to his ancestry, "we've got to have more than one of them at the party. As many as possible, in fact. Get him along—tell him all kinds of enticing lies and if you have to, promise him a gaming room from say midnight on. But for goodness' sake, don't let him carry any—ugh—*lice* along with him!"

"Do you want to tell Harold where Joshua's fortune came from?" Sarah whispered, sidling up beside Chester as the group headed for the next room, the one containing Tabitha Freitas.

Chester shook his head. "I'm beginning to feel a little sorry for him," he answered. "I think things are already worse than I ever dreamed they could become."

CHAPTER XIII

Cy Detrick was shivering and sweating at the same time as he was shown into Solomon Schatzenheim's office. He was over six feet, solidly built with a ruddy complexion, but his manner was that of a far smaller man.

Solomon glowered at him under beetling brows and motioned him to sit down. He said, "So you're the man with the interrogation code for Sparky who failed to warn us about this reunion with his ancestors that Freitas is having tonight!"

"Yes, I'm afraid I did miss out on that," Detrick admitted, surreptitiously wiping his hands on the sides of his shorts to get rid of the sticky perspiration which made his palms itch. "But I hope to show that I can more than make up for it."

"*I* hope so," Solomon said meaningly. "Well, say your piece and hurry up about it. I have to go catch a plane for Arizona in a few minutes."

"Well, sir, it's about these nine ancestors that Mr Freitas is—uh—planning to put on display this evening. To find out who the most suitable candidates were, he hired a genealogist called Flannagan, and I've spent the past couple of days pumping him surreptitiously. I had to lay out quite a lot in drinks and—"

"If what you've come up with is worth knowing, you'll have your expenses refunded. Go on."

"Yes, sir. Well, he was perfectly open about the fact that he sometimes pretties up the biographical data about his clients' ancestors. He doesn't seem to have realized yet that the real people are going to be shown off at this here party; he's sort of treating the whole thing as a joke. That is, he did so until I pointed out he was likely to be sued for fraud on the strength of the doctored biographies he'd fed to Freitas. Then he went all soft and anxious, and I—uh—well, I promised him legal aid if he helped me a bit."

"Come to the point, damn it!" Solomon rasped.

"Yes, sir. Well, I started at the most recent end of the list, of course, because as far as I can make out the ones from way way back probably don't even speak recognizable English, and I came up with all this terrific dirt on them. Here!" He passed a fat folder across Solomon's desk.

"A lot of that can be confirmed just by going to a regular library computer and punching the right codes; the information is all in store but it's been kind of soft-pedaled. For instance, you'll see in there that Buffalo Hank Freitas was wanted in Dodge City, Denver and Abilene at the time he was shot out in Fresno, where he'd run off to avoid charges of trading arms and whisky to the Indians. Then there's his aunt Tabitha, the so-called Civil War heroine who gave refuge to all these Union soldiers and trapped a Confederate force and handed them over to the North complete with their colonel and was honored with this reception at the White House after the war. Well, the reason the White House reception isn't recorded in the official annals took a while to locate, but in the end I found it in a collection of memoirs written a few years later. Apparently Major-General Gaskin, who was one of Sherman's staff officers, had talked to some of Tabitha Freitas's slaves while he was billeted there and found out that a certain alleged rape committed on her by a Confederate officer was nothing of the kind. Nor was it the first. She'd also told the Confederate officer that she'd been raped by his predecessor from the North. So Gaskin marched up to her in the middle of the ballroom and slapped her face with his glove, calling her a whore at the top of his voice. It was a considerable scandal. She appears to have been a thoroughgoing nymphomaniac."

Solomon's eyes were gleaming. "Carry on, Mr Detrick," he purred. "But I already know I'm looking forward to the Freitas reunion party, after all."

Detrick stifled a sigh of relief. "Then there's the senator," he said. "Er—Horatio Freitas, who commanded the *Jolie Marjolaine* during the War of Independence. According to the majority of history books, he was taken ill at the age of forty-five and spent the rest of his life in retirement at his country estate. True enough as far as it goes, but the nature of the illness isn't generally mentioned. He was a paranoid, convinced that every stranger who came to call was a British agent out to assassinate him. In the end, he shot and nearly killed a perfectly respectable landowner called Robbins who was apparently lobbying him for some sort of support in connection with a bill then before the Senate. It was efficiently hushed up because naturally no one at the time wanted it noised around that a great naval hero had gone out of his mind, but I managed to track down some legal papers referring to the damages paid out of court to Robbins to keep the secret. It was a stinging sum for those days, about five thousand dollars."

"More?" Solomon inquired, not attempting to conceal the greed in his voice.

"Well, sir, naturally the further back you go, the more difficult it is to pin down the documentary evidence, but there's Ebenezer, who was responsible for the death of several of the poor devils killed during the Salem witch hunt, allegedly including his own daughter, and then of course there's . . ."

"This is a personal request from the President," Louisa Fold said unhappily to Harold. "He particularly wants to meet Horatio Freitas tonight, because no honor could be greater than to shake the hand of a man who has shaken hands with Washington, the father of his country."

Harold shrank a little in his chair.

"This is from the Daughters of the American Revolution, via your second cousin once removed Mrs Anita Freitas Brown, who think that apart from being the only lady out of the nine of your ancestors who have been summoned to the present—I quote—'Tabitha Freitas is among that noble handful of warrior women who have upheld the ideals of our country for later generations to admire and emulate.' "

"But whether or not she actually was a heroine, she's simply not fit to be put on display!" Harold groaned. "Why, I thought I was lucky to get out of there without being raped! I never saw such a pair of bedroom eyes in my entire life!"

"Yes," Louisa said, and allowed a short silence to

stretch until it was nearly intolerable. Then she resumed, turning up the next in the thick stack of special requests from notable personalities which she had before her.

"This is from Chief Rocket Bomb of the Seshawawa Indians, who says that he is eager to make the acquaintance of Buffalo Hank. He says his great-grandfather used to tell how Buffalo Hank smoked the pipe of peace with *his* great-grandfather, Medicine Tent."

"How pleased is he going to be when he hears Buffalo Hank boasting about the scalps he collected while they were building the Grand Pacific Railroad?" Harold demanded rhetorically. Louisa didn't even attempt to answer, but thumbed up the next paper from the pile.

"This is from the first secretary of the British Embassy in Washington—you remember, it turned out that his grandmother was a Freitas, so we invited him. He says that Joshua's son, Lionel, was twice MP for his home city of Liverpool, so could he possibly put in a special request to be introduced to Joshua tonight? He wants to invite him to an embassy banquet next week and he's promising to lay on a civic reception for Joshua when he's checked with the present lord mayor of Liverpool."

Harold winced visibly. "Is that the lot?" he inquired in an optimistic tone.

"Not by a long chalk, I'm afraid. Here's one from the dean of Freitas College, Freitas, Ohio, the horse-and-buggy town they named for the street in Winchester, Massachusetts, where its founder was born. Apparently about the only department they can boast with a decent academic standard is the Department of Medieval Music—they managed to snag some unworldly German expert on the subject and he's been there for the past ten years bringing all kinds of reflected glory to them. You can guess who they're after, can't you?"

"About the only thing that could make *that* worse," Harold said gloomily, "would be if the dean turned out to be fabulously handsome and of—uh—Greek inclinations. Is he?"

"It's a woman, over sixty and extremely fat. I checked."

"Hmm! Not that we know for sure that makes any difference to the Earl of Winchelsea. Go on, tell me the worst."

"We've had the worst, I think," Louisa said judiciously. "Unfortunately, we haven't by any means had the lot. Here's another, this time from the moderator of the Combined Methodist, Episcopalian, Congregationalist, Baptist and Unitarian Churches of North America Ecumenical Conference Standing Committee on Interfaith Relations and Policy Evaluation."

"Oh, lord. Don't tell me *he's* a Freitas, too?"

"Not exactly, but he makes it pretty clear that we can only look forward to a favorable verdict on the propriety of timescooping people from the past provided we allow one of his leading associates to meet Ebenezer. That's Mrs Adelina Freitas-Lockerby-Horn, Grand Crested Cockatoo of the Sisters of the Southern Order of Neo-Chivalry from Memphis, Tennessee."

"And if we don't play along?"

"They'll condemn the technique as blasphemous, I guess." She turned the next paper up. "Oh, that one's fairly innocuous—it's from the makers of Gloriana Tobacco who want Edgar to write them a sonnet on the virtues of their cigarettes. It's the only request for Edgar, actually, and there won't be anyone from the company at the party tonight, though there may well be a few shareholders we ought to appease."

"The one genuinely presentable person out of the nine, and nobody at the party who especially wants to meet him," Harold said bitterly. "I'm beginning to feel that the universe is plotting against me. Any more, blast it?"

"Hundreds." Louisa shrugged. "I'm simply giving you samples, one for each of the nine ancestors they're expecting to meet. Here's one for Sir Godwin, which is particularly embarrassing, I'm afraid. It's from Ishmael ibn-Abdallah of the New Reformed Orthodox Mosque of Genuine Islam, Incorporated—you know, the one who bore 'Freitas' as what they call a 'slave name' and gave it up on his conversion. He says that Sir Godwin was one of the first people to recognize that the day of the white Christian is over and did a great service to the forerunners of the Black Muslim movement, the Saracens. It's obviously meant to be sarcastic as hell, but he wields far too much influence for us simply to ignore the request."

Harold mentally reviewed the list of the nine ancestors. "So what have you got for Sieur Bohun—another nasty little snare?"

"Very nasty," Louisa sighed. "Count Alfonso de Freitas de Aragon y de Harpalus, the one who's coming down specially for the reunion from the Spanish colony on the Moon, has a bee in his bonnet. He thinks the comet depicted in the Bayeux tapestry actually represents the landing of an alien spaceship and the creatures from the ship, not the Normans, conquered England. He insists on being allowed to interrogate Sieur Bohun right away about the planet from which he originated."

"With hypnosis, truth drugs, all that kind of thing?"

"Judging from the hectoring tone of this note here," Louisa muttered, "with whips, bludgeons and hot irons would be more like it!"

Harold put his head in his hands. "How in the world did I ever let myself be pushed into this mess?" he muttered.

"Correction, Mr Freitas," said the calm voice of Sparky, who had as usual been sitting in on the discussion. Harold glanced up scowling at the impassive Voltaire mask on the screen next to Louisa's.

"What kind of correction?" he rasped.

"Mrs Sarah Freitas, Dr Chester Waley and others of your staff expressed strong reservations about—"

"Oh, go to hell!" Harold roared. Then: "Cancel that! I need help. I need advice. Suppose we just don't let these ancestors of mine show up at the party tonight?"

"Freitas Interplanetary's credibility gap will widen by five hundred percent within the next twenty-four hours," Sparky said.

"And if we do let these—these nut cases and nymphomaniacs loose among my guests?"

"There will be a sharp downturn in the favorable rating of Freitas Interplanetary's image among the public at large, but nothing like so violent—perhaps of the order of ten or twelve percent of the recently accrued gain, which itself amounts to forty percent of the base rating."

"Then you'll just have to tell me how to get off lightest," Harold said, sighing. "Come on—let's be hearing from you."

CHAPTER XIV

With perfect composure, Sarah Freitas awaited the arrival of her guests on the vast platform overhanging the abyss of the Grand Canyon. She was exquisite in black shot through with golden threads that matched her hair to within .005 on the Pansystem Colormatch Scale; she was the very image of a society hostess in the mid-twenty-first century.

Alongside her, Harold was almost chattering his teeth with apprehension, even though he had assured her five or six times already that every possible precaution had been taken and Sparky himself had supervised the last-minute revisions to the program for the festivities which were designed to reduce inevitable mishaps to a minimum.

"Cool it a little, Harold," Sarah whispered as the first of the distant members of the Freitas clan emerged from the main entrance, oohing and aahing at the spectacle before them. Harold Freitas I, casting around for something to spend the surplus of his colossal fortune on, had hit on the notion of offering to restore the Grand Canyon to the condition it had been in when the first explorers visited it, and maintaining it so against the right to use it up to four times a year in perpetuity for a party at one of its most scenic rapids. Inflatable changing rooms, rest rooms and overnight accommodations lined the brink on either side; below them, cunningly sited lights emphasized the marvelous rock formations, and a web of silent air-driven elevators in transparent tubes gave access to fifty platforms secured to the sides of the canyon, some with bars on them, some with buffets, some with dance bands in various styles, some with couches and armchairs, some with swimming pools, some with erotic three-vee shows. The variety was almost endless.

Far below this entrance level, the river itself cascaded over harsh rocks, the sound echoing faintly upwards by way of ingenious conduits so that even here, hundreds of feet higher, one was never able to forget the presence of the natural force that had carved this immense gulf from the living rock.

Fresh from what Sarah was sure must have been a daunting encounter with reporters at the afternoon press conference, Chester stood next to her as being the leader of the Timescoop team, apparently quite calm and impeccably dressed in dark red, which went well with his complexion. Beyond him was the honorary dowager of the Freitas clan, Mrs Honoria Crub, née Freitas, who was nearly a hundred and surviving only on daily geriatric injections, but too notable a figure to be omitted from the reception committee. Beyond her again were a handful of relatively outstanding members of the family, such as the first secretary from the British Embassy. This was one of the last-minute revisions Sparky had recommended. The original plan had been for the nine ancestors to be in this line; now, the scheme was to bring them in later, to set them down at the banquet tables and have them introduced in a speech by Harold after the meal and before the party.

Somewhere out there in the brilliantly colored bubbles of the inflatable temporary buildings, they were currently being talked to, soothed, tranquilized, gentled into acceptable clothing (of their own respective periods, naturally) and otherwise readied for the ordeal ahead. So far, over the ultraminiaturized sound-only radios which both she and Harold wore concealed in their high-fashionable coiffures, the news had been fairly good. Sir Godwin, for instance, had promised to say nothing about his grand plan for ridding Earth of its Mohammedans after a long and hard-to-follow argument with a priest specially fetched from the Aquinas Seminary at Syracuse, New York; Sarah rather had the impression that the poor crusader's head had been left spinning with the ingenuity of the theologian's casuistry, but never mind that—the result was what counted.

Also an extremely unorthodox, but remarkably effective technique involving the services of volunteers from the Society for Absolute Orgasm appeared to have sated Tabitha's desires for the time being. Joshua, once he had been made to understand that he was invited to attend the contemporary equivalent of Beau Nash's soirées at Bath in the company of many of the modern world's most outstanding gentlefolk, had posed no further problems at all; what had eventually won him over was the discovery that a stock of activated syntholon not only could not be creased by careless tying but actually shed dirt while it was being worn, thus maintaining its pristine whiteness indefinitely. According to the harassed Helen Whymore, who was going to be among the later arrivals at the party by the look of things, he regarded this as a tremendous achievement and the perfect proof that there had been progress since his own day.

In fact, the only one out of the whole lot—bar Buffalo Hank, who was three parts drunk on rye whisky, but could be sobered up in five minutes when they got around to giving him a shot of neutralc—who was still posing major problems was Ebenezer. It looked as though he was going to have to be left by himself in one of the changing rooms; he resolutely refused to have any commerce with agents of the devil and as of that morning had decided that even taking food and water was liable to imperil his immortal soul.

"How are you feeling, Chester?" Sarah whispered as she donned the appropriate smile to greet the first of the reunited Freitases, a grocery-store manager from Long Island and his overdressed wife.

"Fractionally better than I ever dared hope," Chester whispered back.

Fifteen minutes after the theoretical starting time, Louisa Fold sorted out the last complaint from the news media—an objection from Jovian Moons Reporting Agency concerning the inferior spot they had been given for their long-range mikes—wiped her forehead covertly and seized a drink off a passing dumbwaiter. There was one hour allowed for people to arrive, and for the fifty most important of them to be presented to the host, hostess and senior staff lined up at the entrance. The rest would have to take their chances. Then there was a thirty-minute allowance for moving to the banquet platform, the largest of the fifty cantilevered out from the wall of the canyon. By the sound of the planes humming overhead, waiting in the stack for permission to set down on the Freitases' private field half a mile away, that half hour wasn't going to be strictly necessary; everyone seemed to be arriving sharp on time —more or less.

The meal itself was, of course, to be served automatically; the five courses accompanied with four different wines would be got through in roughly seventy-five minutes. Then there was to be a short speech by Harold (drafted and timed by Sparky) introducing each of the nine ancestors—correction, eight, if they still hadn't managed to sweeten Ebenezer. After which the gathering would break up and develop into an ordinary party lasting until dawn, with special arrangements to ensure that there was continuous coverage of the ancestors when they met contemporary public figures.

It was going to call for neat timing, naturally; if any son-of-a-skunk reporter insisted on covering the encounter between Sir Godwin and Ishmael ibn-Abdallah, for example, when he could have been paying attention to Joshua and the British Embassy official, or Edgar and the various professors of literature who had been encouraged to request an introduction to him, then that was one three-vee service which could go whistle for Freitas advertising from now on!

Compared to what Louisa would have forecast if she had spoken her mind frankly at noon that day, though, it looked as though it was going to go off relatively smoothly.

She glanced hurriedly at herself in the self-lighted mirror of the compact dangling from her right wrist, decided she was remarkably tidy after so much strain, gulped the drink she had taken and headed for the group at the entrance to the party.

Just before the one-hour mark was reached, Miriam and Solomon Schatzenheim walked—or, as far as Solomon was concerned, perhaps "marched" was a better term—across the main platform. Solomon was trying not to scowl thunderously, and failing.

Shaking Harold's hand, he said with murderous sweetness, "Well, Harold! I have to admit that this time you really put one over on us!"

Harold, brightening noticeably, returned the handshake with excessive enthusiasm.

"It's such a shame, isn't it, that your ancestors have turned out on close acquaintance to be such unsavory characters? Still, no one can help who his forefathers were, can he? I suppose among my own progenitors there must have been the odd black sheep, and it's very brave of you to face that risk and actually employ your astonishing Timescoop for this reunion."

One fraction of a second before Harold blew his top, Sarah cut in, hurrying to embrace Miriam. "My dear! How wonderful that you were able to come! And Solomon—how nice! Yes, you're absolutely right about Harold's ancestors, aren't you? As they say, great gifts and great faults go together—but naturally you'll have the chance to see that for yourself later on this evening. I don't believe you've met Chester Waley, have you? He's really the person responsible for the great success of Timescoop, the leader of the technical research team which conducted the initial experiments."

Babbling nineteen to the dozen, she contrived to shuffle the Schatzenheims along the line. Just as the Secret Service agents preceding the President himself came striding through the entrance, she whispered to Harold, "I told you to cool it! Stop imagining the worst is going to happen—your ancestors can't have been totally stupid, and they must have some vestige of what passed for social graces in their own time! The moment they see this enormous crowd waiting to greet them, they'll probably calm down and behave like lambs for fear of dishonoring the family."

"I only hope you're right," Harold muttered, and composed his face into a smile for the President's benefit.

CHAPTER XV

Following little illuminated bubbles drifting through the air ahead of them, the hundreds of banquet guests took their places at the tables assigned to them and stood expectantly behind their chairs waiting for the long head table, directly against the canyon wall, to fill with its notabilities.

And there they came! Clapping broke out as the knowledgeable whispered names to their neighbors. Harold escorting the First Lady, Louisa Fold with the President, James Quentin with Tabitha, Sarah with the poet Edgar—but why only eight of them in those peculiar ancient costumes, the gown to ankle level, the braided coat, the knee breeches, all the rest of it? A buzz of conversation displaced the applause.

The people at the head table took their places, the President sat down and the vast concourse copied him. The automatic dispensers at each place delivered forced avocados with Martian dressing in individual gilt shells, the plopping sound momentarily drowning out the buzz of voices but only for a second or two. Virtually no one made a move to start eating; most of the company were counting, some actually extending their forefingers and numbering off the ancestors, one, two, three . . .

"Harold!" Sarah hissed into her concealed radio. "Go tell a polite lie to account for Ebenezer's absence! Otherwise, they'll go on staring all night!"

"Ah—okay." Harold sighed, and left his chair in favor of the toastmaster's dais. Over the microphones he said, "It appears that some of you must be wondering about the —ah—the absence of the Reverend Ebenezer Freitas."

"That's the one who's missing!" One could pick the words out clearly from the general babble.

"Well—uh—unfortunately he's indisposed. I'm to convey you his regrets at not being able to be with us."

There were universal nods. Satisfied, Harold returned to his seat—only to notice with dismay that on his far left the Sieur Bohun de Freitas had picked up his avocado pear and was sniffing at it suspiciously.

"What's this—hog's food?" he roared, his high-speed English lessons having taken to such good effect that everyone for twenty places either side heard him clearly. Panicking, Harold gestured for Helen's attention.

"Blazes, of course—in his day they ate practically no vegetables!" she groaned. "I'd forgotten about that. Never mind, I'll just ask for his main dish to be served at once."

A moment later, the offending avocado was removed automatically and Jovian spiced capon garnished with sauté potatoes and salad appeared instead. That was more to Sieur Bohun's liking, although he immediately pitched the vegetables back down the hole they had appeared from—which later caused some problems to the service engineers responsible for maintenance of the delivery system—and put the capon to his mouth whole, careless of the way its gravy ran over his chin.

"At least he seems to approve of the wine," Sarah murmured to her seat neighbor, Edgar. Indeed, not only Sieur Bohun but Sir Godwin and likewise Tabitha had already drained their glasses of dry Bordeaux white and signaled for a refill. "But how about you?" she continued.

Rather pale, Edgar said, "My lady—"

"Edgar, I kept telling you; you address me as Sarah. I'm not a lady!"

"My lady," the boy repeated obstinately. "Not even at Gloriana's court, when she gave her fabled banquets for Sir Walter Raleigh or for Sir Francis Drake, could such marvels have been assembled at one place and one time in the age from which you've haled me hither. This strange and subtle delicacy that you've set before me—is it true that all this vast company is enjoying the same?"

Sarah nodded. There was something very touching about this boy's modesty and desire to please. No—correction. Not a boy. Not in his own day. By eighteen and a half, he might have been captain of a ship of the line; head of a family, with four or five children; administrator and lord of a big estate, with a hundred peasant farmers looking to him for guidance. He was a man in his own eyes, and should be thought of as such.

"And is it a—a plant of the New World where I find myself?"

Sarah had to think twice before answering. "Yes, I suppose it must be," she said at length.

"It's delicious," Edgar muttered, savoring the latest mouthful. "Yet in this New World you speak the tongue of England, and this plant has a Spanish name: *abogado*, lawyer. I would fain know how that came about." He shook his head. "Truly there is much to be learned about this strange and fabulous world you live in!"

"Everything you want to know, you shall be told," Sarah promised, and touched his arm companionably. "But please don't look to me as an encyclopedia."

"As a—what?"

"Blast. Of course, I was forgetting; they didn't invent that word until after your day. Never mind, Edgar. I'm afraid that's not the only new thing you'll have to learn."

"Should I need to be told?" Edgar riposted. "I am almost giddy with the wonders I've been shown already. What makes me marvel perhaps more than all else lies here." He glanced up and down the table and spoke in a lower voice. "Why are not these others, my kinfolk, enthused with the same miracles as am I? While waiting to join the company just now, I spoke a little with them, and 'tis my clear feeling that they would rather not have been shown this great new age. My—my great-nephew, as I think he is, the one called Joshua: he down the table a piece, who wears that fine gold-embroidered coat and sports a gentleman's sword: he is one who seems not to care for the experience."

"He seems to be doing okay at the moment." Sarah shrugged. Indeed, the sight of the vast company appeared to have fulfilled her earlier prediction to Harold in at least one case. Joshua was blossoming. He was—as near as she could tell at this distance—recounting scandalous gossip about the royal family of England in his day, to the huge delight of those closest to him. In particular, he seemed to be taken with Tabitha, seated two places away from him, and they were making eyes at each other continually.

Edgar looked distressed. "He seems to be—what? Your pardon! You must think me extremely ignorant—*Sarah*."

"Not at all." She smiled. "I think you're a darling, to be honest—by far the nicest of all these ancestors of Harold's."

He stared down at the by now empty shell of his avocado. Blushing crimson, he muttered, "It is long past time that I should beg your forgiveness, by the way. When first you stole into my—my quarters to talk with me, I had no faintest idea that you were pledged to . . ."

"Harold is my husband," Sarah said.

"God's wounds!" Edgar dropped his spoon in his agitation. "My lady, I—"

"You have nothing to apologize for. Believe me, nothing. As you yourself said, you have a lot to learn about this new world you've found yourself in. Oh lord, now what's gone wrong?" She craned forward impolitely and stared up the table toward the spot where Harold, the President and his wife, and Senator Horatio Freitas were sitting. There was clearly some sort of disagreement going on.

She touched the lock of hair curling over her right ear which concealed the activating switch of her radio, and whispered, "Harold, what's wrong?"

"Oh, nothing much," the answer came back, Harold's voice recognizably resigned despite the frequency-clipping necessary to carry the words on circuitry much finer than the hair which covered it. "It's a slight attack of the paranoia we were warned about. Horatio just learned that there is someone here from the British Embassy and is convinced that his avocado must be poisoned."

"Lord! Can you do anything to calm him down?"

"I've had to promise that I'll exchange dishes whenever anything appears on the table in front of him. I think that should hold him for a while, at least. Pray he doesn't decide that that's all part of the plot, hm?"

"I see what you mean. Think we're ready to go on to the soup now?"

It was by far the most nerve-racking meal Sarah had ever eaten. There was small comfort to be found in the fact that as yet things were going well for her friend Miriam; by eyebrow-telegraph along the table, she contrived to ask a question and got back an enthusiastic answer, which rendered into words would have gone approximately:

"How's it with you?"

"Fabulous so far! Solomon's hoping against hope that one of the ancestors will create a scene, but the worst that's happened yet is Old Hog's-food over there with his abominable table manners."

Sieur Bohun was definitely the least elegant eater who had ever sat at table with the present generation of Freitases; he had gobbled his way through four of the roast capons by this time—pitching aside the offending vegetables—and he was smeared with grease and gravy almost to the elbows. This head table was covered with a genuine white damask cloth, and he had used that and the skirts of his surcoat indifferently to wipe his fingers on. Little by little his neighbors had drawn away from him to make extra space, and now he was encircled by a kind of miniature rampart of chicken bones, two or three glasses he'd clasped too tightly and cracked, and which had automatically been replaced, and those vegetables he'd aimed at the delivery slot and failed to score a hit with.

Luckily, however, the immense quantities of wine he had poured down his throat were gradually getting the better of him. By the end of the meal there was a good chance he would have dozed off; already his movements were inaccurate and his speech slurred. In Sparky's view, it would cause less distress among the other guests if he got swinishly drunk and passed out than if he remembered about his host bearing the name of the traitor king, Harold, and decided to voice his objections.

The soup course passed off relatively uneventfully, and by the time the salmon mayonnaise succeeded it, Sarah was a trifle more relaxed, though she could never quite forget the stare of all those hundreds of eyes—and beyond them the lenses of the three-vee cameras, relaying this function in real time to a system-wide audience. On impulse she contacted Louisa Fold, who was also wearing one of the concealed radios like hers and Harold's, to ask what the coverage had been like so far.

"Fair," was the succinct reply. "One of the networks has been paying entirely too much attention to Sieur Bohun, but that's presumably because they carry more Schatzenheim advertising than Freitas advertising, and our monitors say the audience is switching off their channel in droves in favor of others which are giving more variety to their coverage. By the way, you and your handsome chum Edgar are drawing a lot of attention, and he's already had more than three hundred proposals of marriage since he first showed on the screens."

"I'm not surprised," Sarah murmured, and cut off.

So the main course and the dessert slipped into memory. As coffee and liqueurs, cigars and cigarettes popped from all the delivery slots except Sieur Bohun's—where they jammed under a soggy mound of potatoes and lettuce—Harold braced himself and glanced around.

Everyone was staring at him, including his ancestors. By the look of it, the therapy administered to Tabitha, radical though it was, had already started to wear off, for the same old glint was in her eyes, but provided she could be cooled down for a little while yet, things would be okay. He gave a prearranged signal, and members of Louisa's PR staff who were being paid heavy bonuses for the indignity of turning up in footmen's uniforms stole silently to stand in pairs behind each ancestor's chair. Outwardly it looked like a splendid and expensive tribute to their presence; actually it was a further precaution recommended by Sparky. They were all palming tiny tranquilizer guns for use in emergency.

"Pray silence for your host!" boomed the voice of the automated toastmaster system, another of Sparky's subsidiary attachments. "The President of Freitas Interplanetary Corporation, Harold Freitas III!"

Harold rose and, amid a raging sea of applause, made his way to the podium. Looking out over all those faces, thinking of the uncountable millions who must be viewing him by way of the three-vee cameras, he felt his heart swell in his chest.

It was working out. Against all the warnings and gloomy forebodings of his staff, of Sarah, of Chester, they had reached the climax of his plan. Even Sieur Bohun had had the grace to fall on his face on the table and he was going to be able to use the second-line joke in the speech Sparky had drafted for him, the one concerning the danger of visiting the garderobe at Bellisle Castle in winter when the wind was below freezing point—a trifle risqué, but not likely to offend a fraction as many people as it would delight.

Let tomorrow bring what it would. For the moment, he was monarch of all he surveyed, the latest of many worthy heads of the Freitas clan, triumphing over all adversity.

"He's getting away with it!" Solomon moaned in the silence of his skull. Outwardly he maintained a perfectly calm expression, but inwardly he was fuming. Why hadn't that son-of-a-bitch Detrick's predictions been fulfilled? Why hadn't Horatio Freitas tried to murder the British Embassy official? Why hadn't Tabitha tried to tear the clothes off her seat neighbor? Why hadn't Buffalo Hank gone after the scalp of one of the many staffers around with Indian ancestry?

It was too late to arrange anything now. But tomorrow—oh, yes! Tomorrow there was going to be trouble!

CHAPTER XVI

"Mr Freitas, it's quite marvelous!" gushed the First Lady as, with the precision of a military operation, the grouping for the banquet was rearranged into the grouping for the subsequent party. "How wonderful to be able to meet someone like Horatio Freitas who shook hands with Washington! And, speaking of meeting people, do you think I could possibly . . . ?"

Buffalo Hank, glowing comfortably from the brandy he had gulped down during the speech Harold had just made, was beginning to think that this incredible new world wasn't such a bad place after all. It was a hell of a sight easier to drift around this Godforsaken hunk of land in these here aircraft, or as he was doing now on these platforms they referred to as "airlevators," than traveling the way he'd had to when he first came out here: on the back of a balky mule. And these here women—hoo boy! After all those years of stinking squaws grimy from campfire smoke, and the occasional dance-hall floozie, seeing so many clean white women was making him tall in the saddle.

He glanced idly to the right as he accompanied his guides into the depths of the canyon, and started. "Hey! What's that going on there?" he yelled.

"We'll show you later, Mr Freitas," was the answer. "Right now you have to meet—"

"Dadblame the son of a coyote I'm supposed to meet! This is where I stop right now! I never saw a show like this before—not even back in the East!"

"I'm terribly sorry, Miss Fold," the harassed PR man said. "The moment he clapped eyes on the erotica show we have going on level fourteen, he pointblank refused to go any farther."

"Oh, lord," Louisa sighed. "Go punch for Sparky and

find out what kind of a polite fiction we can spin to all those frontier-gun buffs who are waiting to talk to him."

"I need to have some blood let," Horatio Freitas insisted. "*I* know what's wrong with me! I'll be damned if I let you pour any of your British poisons down my gullet!"

"Miss Fold," the PR staffer whispered, "it's Horatio this time. He's not feeling too good after the banquet—the doctors think he overate in spite of everything—but he wants to have his blood let and thinks modern medicine is a plot to poison him. It's going to take a while to calm him down."

"Go punch for Sparky and find out what we can tell those D.A.R. delegates who want to meet him. And hurry!"

"You mean you can really kill *millions* of people?" Tabitha said to the Aerospace Force general in his black and silver uniform. "Fantastic! To think of that power resting in one man's hands! And, speaking of hands, general, did anyone ever tell you you have beautiful hands—so strong, so gentle?"

"Miss Fold! We just got the latest psychoportrait of Tabitha through from Sparky. We have her pinned down at last. She gets some kind of extra bang from lovers who are in positions of power, especially those who've exercised power in the crudest way by killing people. Right now she's trying to corner General Wallington."

"Quick—go ask Sparky what we can tell the Civil War buffs waiting on level thirty-six while we cool her down!"

In the distance, Ebenezer Freitas heard music, laughter, merry voices. He maintained his permanent scowl. He hadn't been able to resist being brought to this new department of the infernal regions, but he did at least have the Good Book with him and it was a source of endless consolation.

Bit by bit, though, he was starting to wonder why he had been allowed to retain his Bible. Surely agents of the Evil One should have been terrified of it? As it was, one of them had actually picked it up and handed it to him with a smile.

"The Devil knows the scriptures," he quoted under his breath. That must imply that he was able to read them. But it was small consolation. His belly was beginning to grumble at the lack of food and his throat was parched.

"Ebenezer is still reading quietly by himself," the PR staffer reported.

"Thank goodness there's one of them who isn't giving us any headaches," Louisa said. "Funny it should be the one we expected the worst of."

"Edgar isn't, either," the PR man reassured her. "He's down with Mrs Freitas on level forty-one—the one where we programmed the band with the right kind of music—and he's teaching her some kind of dance. I think it's called a 'galliard.' "

About an hour or so after he passed out, Sieur Bohun woke up again and was extremely sick. But that was in the infirmary building they'd moved him to, so the only people who had to witness the disgusting spectacle were medical staff.

"Why anyone should want to waste money on bringing back a creature like this," one of the nurses muttered, "is completely beyond me!"

Meanwhile, Count Alfonso de Freitas de Aragon y de Harpalus went around loudly assuring everyone who would listen that it was Sieur Bohun's alien metabolism which had betrayed him when he attempted to digest terrestrial food.

"Sir Godwin seems to have offended just about everybody," the PR staffer reported glumly. "Someone let it slip in his hearing that Jerusalem has been internationalized, and he decided it was a God-given chance for him to raise a new crusade. You should have heard the language he used to people who said they had better things to do than go and storm the Holy City!"

"I'm glad I didn't!" Louisa snapped. "Go ask Sparky how we can convince him he's fighting for a lost cause!"

At least, reflected the Earl of Winchelsea and Poitenne, they had given up plaguing him about that damned music they first expected from him. Were all these people of the future out of their minds? Music was something soothing to have in the background while men argued about important matters with key dignitaries—a fit pastime for deranged monks like Clarence, but not something to preoccupy a landed lord!

Granted, his choir had had its uses, but mainly it was a good way of getting little boys away from their apprehensive parents. Also, of course, it attracted clerics, women and other unmanly persons. But it was practically an insult to think that he would prize it above affairs of state!

Not to worry, though. Some things hadn't changed. A neglected wife remained a neglected wife even though it was some incomprehensible commercial venture instead of a decent knightly errand that had taken away her husband. And pressure could doubtless still be applied in the ancient way.

"A psychoportrait of the Earl of Winchelsea just came through. Turns out he's not interested in women, only in wives—especially neglected ones. Right now he's chatting up Miriam Schatzenheim."

"Christ, we'll have to watch that!"

"Not to seduce her. Only to see if he can start some kind of intrigue by playing up to her. *He's* not one of Mr Freitas's ancestors. He couldn't ever have been anyone's ancestor. He's one hundred percent pedophile, and proud of it."

"But according to the record—"

"He must have allowed himself to be cuckolded for the sake of an heir. Sparky says the genotypes confirm it; it's out of the question for him to be the father of the boy he claimed as his son."

"For God's sake, don't tell Mr Freitas until after the party, then!"

His spirits rising a little, Chester Waley wandered from level to level of the party, occasionally exchanging greetings with fellow scientists and almost as often having to extricate himself from reporters who had managed to elude the security guards and mingle with the throng. Both wanted details of the Timescoop technique which his contract forbade him to talk about.

At the back of his mind was a vague idea that it would be salutary to send for a selection of the pioneer scientists who had tried and failed to establish an international camaraderie transcending not merely commercial rivalries but even the demands of patriotism. There were so many people, including two or three here at the party, with whom he wanted to discuss the implications of Timescoop, yet he dared not do so.

Accordingly, it had occurred to him to track down Joshua, whose—ah—*former* existence had overlapped the so-called Age of Reason, who had shared a century with, for instance, the philosophers of the Lunatic Society. He might have some data to indicate how those brilliant but informal experimenters got away with it in face of what could not have been much less frustrating obstacles.

He passed level after level, noting the presence of various of the ancestors: Buffalo Hank roaring with delight at the erotic show he was monopolizing, letting off his blank-charged six-guns at every climax in the performance; Edgar instructing Sarah and a dozen envious girls in the steps of some complex formal dance. . . .

And, eventually, there was Joshua, holding forth to a fascinated audience that included major public figures: a congressman, a university professor, a society hostess from Washington, and many more. For a while, Chester hung around on the fringe of the crowd, listening to the incontestably witty—although unprintable—scandal Joshua was retailing about the famous of his own day, up to and including royalty. Then came his chance to break in, as several of the listeners decided simultaneously to go look for more to drink.

"Ah—Mr Joshua Freitas! I wonder if I might have a

word with you?" he exclaimed, advancing and holding out his hand to be shaken.

"And what makes you think a gentleman would wish to talk to you?" returned Joshua, obviously drunk but bright-eyed and clear of speech. "You're a black, damn it! You're not for talking to—you're for buying and selling!"

The world seemed to stop dead. Chester heard himself say very distinctly, "I beg your pardon?"

"Granted. Go away, nigger—I've shipped your kind by the thousand across the Atlantic, and small profit I had of it, what with so many of you dying on the voyage and cheating me out of my dividends. Go back to your mud hut, or whatever it is you live in, and leave me alone."

He deliberately turned his back. Chester, in the grip of a fury he had not known since he was a child, a blind fury that made the world turn red, strode up to him, seized him by the shoulder and spun him around.

"Are you boasting of the money you made from slaves?" he rasped.

Joshua shook free and spun to face him. He looked paradoxically delighted.

"Why not?" he purred. "What else are niggers good for?"

Chester drew back his right fist and slammed it forward again. It took Joshua under the chin. He rocked and almost fell, but not quite. He said, "Just as I'd have expected—the action of a savage, not a gentleman!"

"So what would a 'gentleman' do in your view?" Chester snapped.

"Why, settle the dispute in an honorable fashion!" Joshua touched the sword at his side meaningly. "But to become involved with a black man—no, it's unthinkable!"

"You're involved, whether you like it or not," Chester said. He felt a little giddy, but the words came pouring out before he could check them, driven by a lifetime-long hatred for the men who had bought and sold his ancestors like merchandise. "And since you think I can't behave like a gentleman, I'll go along with you. I'm going to tear those fancy breeches off you and whale your ass until you scream for mercy!"

"Mr Frietas! Mr Freitas! *Quickly!*"

"Excuse me, Mr President. Yes, Louisa, what do you want, damn it?"

"Down on level forty-five—it's Joshua! He picked some kind of a quarrel with Chester Waley and insisted on a duel to settle it. And—!"

"And what?"

"And someone *gave* Chester a sword and Joshua was so drunk he ran straight in on the point of it. He's dead, and the doctors can't revive him. They're sending for the police right now!"

CHAPTER XVII

"But where on earth did you find the sword you used?" Harold moaned, rocking back and forth on his heels. Sitting opposite him in a high-backed chair, Chester, who was visibly trembling from shock, gave a sigh.

"Apparently it was Edgar's," he muttered. "One of the PR staffers who'd been assigned to ride herd on Joshua dashed up to fetch it from the level where he was dancing with Sarah. He'd taken it off because it was getting in the way, and—"

"But for pity's sake, Chester, what got into you to do such a crazy thing?" Harold appealed with his eyes to the encircling group—Sarah, Helen, Quentin, the doctor who had tried and failed to save Joshua's life—for their agreement that it was a crazy act.

"I've told you!" Chester snapped. "When I first discovered from Sparky that Flannagan had lied to you about Joshua making his fortune from the sugar trade, I was on the verge of turning in my resignation. He ran cargoes to Jamaica and Barbados, all right—or rather his agents did—but sugar and rum were just the things they filled the holds with for the return voyage.

"Then I calmed down a bit, and I told myself that it wasn't really his direct responsibility—he spent most of his time living it up in Bath and London and he couldn't have been the only one of his type and, perhaps, on closer acquaintance he might even turn out to be a decent person with some germ of conscience, after all. When he refused to talk to me, though, because he said niggers were for buying and selling—" He swallowed hard. "I saw red. Literally. It was awful."

"The psychoportrait we've raised for him says he's the sort of man who goes out of his way to pick quarrels," Helen put in. "If we hadn't had to hurry through the acculturation process for all nine of the ancestors in only five days, we'd have had adequate psychoportraits in advance instead of while they were already mingling with the crowd of guests tonight. But we ought to have deduced it ourselves, anyway. He was ready enough to talk about the number of times he'd defended his so-called honor."

She turned away, looking miserable.

"Well, who the hell was this PR staffer who went and fetched the sword?" Harold demanded. "Louisa? Damnation, where is that woman?"

"Getting everyone off the premises with the least fuss," Sarah said.

"Well, don't let this bastard go along with the rest! Quentin, send someone to locate him and hold him until the police arrive! Chester, do you know his name?"

Chester shook his head dispiritedly.

"Can you at least describe him?" Harold pressed.

"Oh—big man, solidly built, dark hair, ruddy face. With a sort of fawning manner."

"I know who you mean," Quentin said. "His name's Cyrus Detrick. He's worked for me on one or two releases concerning research projects. That must be who you mean—a man who seems small even though he's bigger than I am."

"Get after him, then! No, wait—I must be out of my mind. What am I wearing a radio for?" Harold put his hand up to activate the switch hidden in his hair, but Sarah forestalled him.

"I'm already in touch with Louisa," she said, fingering her own switch and listening with an abstracted expression. "What was that, Louisa?"

They waited tensely. After a moment she said, "Hell and damnation. Harold, they already missed him. Directly the trouble broke, they ordered the—ah—the flunkeys to round up your ancestors and get them to the changing rooms or somewhere out of the way. Detrick didn't report to help with the job. They'll go on looking for him, but she didn't sound very optimistic. I think this can't have been an accident."

"Blazes, of course, it can't have been an accident! More like someone out to sabotage my success who seized the opportunity when it was offered. Chester, Chester, why in hell did you do such a stupid thing as to accept his challenge?"

Chester rose to his feet, clenching his fists. "Listen, you smug honky," he said between his teeth. "You're so stinking proud of your ancestors you turned what ought to be a scientific miracle into a goddamned publicity stunt, and here they all are—earls and knights and senators and lord knows what! And what did your ancestors do to *my* ancestors? They kidnapped them, that's what! They penned them up in the filthy holds of slaveships and they cursed them for dying on the way across the ocean because it meant they didn't have so much profit to throw away at the gaming tables! I've used up all my self-control—I warn you. You ask me one more time, you just *breathe* a hint of that idiot question about why I wanted a chance to get level with that dirty son-of-a-bitch Joshua, and I swear I'll write the answer on your face with hydrofluoric acid, mirrorwise around so you can read it every day of your life in the bathroom and remember. Is that clear?"

He shook off Sarah's restraining hand and glowered into Harold's eyes from inches' distance. For a second, Harold tried to meet that accusing glare. He failed and had to turn away.

"I'm sorry," he said, the words muffled.

"Hell of a lot of good that is!" Chester barked, and dropped back in his chair.

"Chester's quite right," Sarah said. "It's done, and what we have to do now is make the best of it. To start with, any court on the continent is bound to accept a plea of intolerable provocation—I've talked to a couple of people who were present on level forty-five when all this happened, and they're prepared to swear that Joshua did refuse to treat Chester as a human being. One of them said he was so angry at what Joshua said he nearly went for him himself, but he decided Chester ought to be allowed to teach him a lesson."

"But how could it have happened so quickly?" Harold demanded. "I thought the whole thing about duels was that they were very formal; you set a time and place, you chose your seconds, you—"

"It went on for a bit after the first insult he made," Chester said dully. "After he'd called me a—a *thing* to be bought and sold and I threatened to tear off his fancy pants and whop his ass for him, he came back with something about my not having any friends to act as my seconds, and then someone from the crowd tried to break in, and I was still blind furious, and then—what did you say his name was? Detrick?—whoever it was, anyway, this flunkey done up in footman's gear just thrust the sword into my hand and, seeing it, Joshua drew his own and people screamed and jumped out of the way and he came at me flailing because he must have been very drunk and—" He put his head in his hands.

"Hell, I was just holding the sword out in front of me, that's all! I never had a sword in my hand in my life before, except like an antique, a museum piece. And I guess he lost his footing on something which had got spilled —a drink maybe, an ice cube, *I* don't know. And there he was, spiked on the end of my sword like a butterfly on a pin, looking so goddamned astonished it was almost funny, until the blood started to bubble out of his mouth."

There was an interlude of silence so complete that the faint, faint sound of someone calling Harold over his scalp-radio was as shocking as an earthquake. "That's the police turning up," he said when he had listened for a moment. "Louisa says she's bringing them straight down to this level. And practically all the guests have been cleared out by now except the ones who actually saw it happening. Most of them are in the infirmary building being treated for shock, but apparently they'll be all right in time to answer the necessary questions."

His face had gone perfectly gray, and he looked more like a corpse himself than Joshua had when they drew the decent concealing sheet over him a quarter hour before.

"Good work, Detrick," Solomon Schatzenheim said over his shoulder directly his plane had shifted from the local control serving Freitas's private field to the state-wide routing computer.

"Th-thank you, Mr Schatzenheim," Detrick whispered from the baggage compartment at the back where he had crouched in order to elude detection while they were taking off. "Is it safe for me to come out now? It's pretty damned cramped in here."

"I guess so." Solomon shrugged and, as Detrick cautiously unfolded himself, glanced at the frozen face of his wife in the adjacent seat.

"What are you looking so miserable for? Harold Freitas brought the whole thing on himself, didn't he, with his greed for publicity?"

"Someone was killed," Miriam said, not looking her husband's way. "You may find that amusing. I don't."

"Not amusing. Satisfactory. Very satisfactory. And you certainly can't accuse me of having arranged it all. It was purely and simply the result of Freitas's stupidity."

Uncertain whether he should intrude on this marital disagreement, Detrick hesitated at the exit from the baggage compartment.

"You come here and sit down," Solomon invited. "A drink, a smoke? If anyone can claim any credit for what just happened, you can. You did some very quick thinking."

Miriam rose from her seat and headed for the toilets at the rear of the plane.

"I prefer not to stay in the same place as someone who's just facilitated a homicide!" she snapped as she pushed past Detrick. "If I had a parachute, I'd jump out!"

"You'll get over it, darling," Solomon said. "Come on, Detrick, sit down and name your poison."

Detective Commander Alfred Helnick, a portly and dignified man in his early sixties, listened impassively to the testimony of the various witnesses while his six identically garbed forensic technicians inspected Joshua's body and the weapon which had brought about his death. His conversation consisted chiefly of grunts and nods for someone else to start talking, until the technicians finished their work and came to stand before him in a semicircle to report.

"Well?" he said.

"Deceased is a white male of thirty-three to thirty-five.

Death is due to a stab wound in the region of the solar plexus resulting in cessation of the breathing reflex, acute shock entailing immediate vagal inhibition and loss of large quantities of blood. The blood on the sword matches up and so does the shape of the wound. So do the prints and epidermal secretion traces. It looks as though they're telling the truth."

"Ah-hah. Thanks." And, as the technicians dispersed again, Helnick continued: "In that case, Dr—it is Dr, yes? —Dr Waley, I'm going to have to place you under arrest on a charge of culpable homicide."

"Chester, don't worry!" Harold said eagerly. "We'll get you the best defense the corporation can afford."

"One moment, please, Mr Freitas," Helnick cut in. "I hadn't finished. I'm also going to accept pro tem and without prejudice to later judicial findings that there's a *prima facie* defense to the effect that Dr Waley was intolerably provoked. So I'm going to apply for an injunction to make sure you don't let these barbarians out of the past loose among decent contemporary folk again. Pending that injunction, I'd advise you to shut them up securely and post a strong armed guard around them."

"What?" Harold blinked in dismay. "But—!"

"No *buts*, if you please. You can try arguing with the judge if you want to; that's your privilege. But in view of what's happened so far as a result of your imbecilic publicity stunt, I think I can predict which of us he's going to listen to without having to consult a computer for its opinion about the outcome."

CHAPTER XVIII

Far in the distance they were deflating the temporary buildings that had been set up for the party. The multi-colored lights all around them were still on; in the glow they looked like flowers dying in accelerated motion, or perhaps more like fungi.

Sarah stood at the window of their country home and listened to the agitated complaints of Harold as he paced up and down behind her.

"But we can't pen them up like animals indefinitely, no matter what that bastard of a policeman says! Lord, the whole idea was that from tomorrow on they should be made available for study, sent out to universities, allowed to go to all the parties and meetings and things people want to lay on for them! If we shut them up—"

"I know what's wrong with you," Sarah said with an air of having reached a tremendous peak of insight.

"What?" Distracted from the flow of his tirade, Harold blinked at her.

"I said I know what's wrong with you," Sarah repeated, and turned to face him. "Lord, have I ever been blind!"

"I—I don't quite . . ." Once again the sensation Harold had hoped to lose forever had him in its grip: the feeling that in some way he was inferior to his wife.

"Harold, dear!" She walked over to him, her face eloquent of compassion, and took his hand comfortingly. "Who's the most distinguished of your ancestors over the last hundred years?"

"I—I guess my grandfather."

"Exactly. But you never even considered bringing him back, did you?"

"Why . . ." Harold looked astonished. "No, I never did think of that!" And he tried, but failed, to control a shudder at the idea.

"Come and sit down," Sarah urged, tugging him gently toward a nearby lounge. "Oh, that damned genealogist! I didn't like him the first time I met him—but I have to admit he's a good pragmatic psychologist. You relied on his recommendations, didn't you?"

"From start to finish." Harold's face darkened. "And when our legal department gets through with him, he'll—"

"Never mind him. He doesn't matter. He played on your own shortcomings. *He* realized that, if he suggested your grandfather as one of the top ten of your ancestors, you'd think back to your own knowledge of him and remember his failings as well as his virtues. You've told me often enough what a brute he could be when he lost his temper!"

"Lord, yes!"

"Well, look. Obviously Flannagan was hoping for some kind of well-paid commission from you; he wanted to keep you enthusiastic about the idea of digging into your genealogy. He can't have known about Timescoop, but perhaps he anticipated being able to send profitable expeditions to England to hunt through moldering parish registers and turn Somerset House upside down and all the rest of it. My guess is that almost up to the last moment he did intend to include your grandfather in the list he recommended to you as outstanding personalities, and then thought better of it. Which is why he gave you nine instead of the ten names you originally asked for."

"So what?" Harold demanded aggressively.

"So if you'd had the idea of bringing back your grandfather shoved under your nose, you'd have had the sense to start thinking about your ancestors as human beings with human faults instead of as tributes to your own importance."

"That's not fair," Harold said sullenly.

"Oh, Harold, I'm not blaming you! I like you—I always have liked you as a person since we first met, or I'd never have agreed to marry you. But when you were suddenly dumped in the top board chair at Freitas Interplanetary, you seemed to change somehow; ever since, you've been permanently bewildered. *I* know how much store you set on this grand family reunion coming out as you planned—who better? But you must admit, what you were really after was having your famous forebears express their gratitude toward you for bringing them back from the dead. Isn't that true?"

"I—" Harold bit back his instinctively angry retort. After a moment he gave a dejected nod.

With a sudden access of spirit, he added, "But you were pretty enthusiastic about it yourself, weren't you?"

Sarah bit her lip. "Yes, I—ah—I hoped that finding yourself up against people from a more vigorous age would make you take fresh stock of yourself. But I never thought it would come out the way it actually has done. Oh, I wish I could make myself as clear as I want to!"

She leaned closer to him. "It goes something like this. You brought me that statue, remember? A present to mark the first successful operation of the Timescoop. And I was dreadfully patronizing about it, wasn't I?"

"Yes," Harold said without the least hint of apology for his bluntness.

She flushed a little, but continued in a steady voice, "And didn't you think of your ancestors the same way—as presents to yourself?"

Harold sat gloomily silent.

"But a person isn't a statue, can't be treated like one. Which was the whole point of trying to recoup your research expenditure by bringing in people instead of *objets d'art*."

"You could stop rubbing my nose in it," Harold muttered.

"No, I can't," Sarah insisted. "I have this clear impression that you hadn't thought beyond tonight; for months you've been concentrating on showing off your famous forebears, and just about all you've done by way of preparation for tomorrow and the day after has been to make this glib generalization about—oh—sending them to universities and letting them go to parties and receptions in their honor."

She jumped up and began to pace the floor in her turn.

"You've been clinging so desperately to this original

idea of yours that you never faced the risk that things might go wrong as they have done. You've never considered just how *new* all this is! I mean—oh—suppose you'd invented the airplane and you were all set to make the first flight in front of witnesses: wouldn't you be prepared for a failure, a mistake, an apology?"

Harold gave a reluctant nod. "But what's the good of recriminating now? I mean there's been a killing, and the whole matter's been taken out of my hands."

"The hell it has," Sarah said. She halted before him and set her hands on her hips. "Harold Freitas, do you care about me? Do you want to go on being married to me?"

"Heavens, yes!" He blinked up at her like a shy teenager. "You're about the only really good thing that ever happened to me, even though I've always wished—"

"Wished what?"

"Wished I could do something to impress you, damn it!"

"I thought that was at the bottom of it. So I guess I owe you an apology for being remote and cynical and—and whatever else I've done in the past. But it's *you* I like, not your damned family or your grandfather's billions or anything else, and I think it's as much your fault as mine that you've wound up feeling the way you do. You've been competing against the past, and that's a contest no one can win because the past has all the advantages. We've forgotten its fiddling little drawbacks: the lice, the skin infections, the disgusting personal habits and the rest of it. Well, you've been instrumental in bringing them back to us, so it's up to you to sort out the consequent problems. And don't give me that bit about the matter having been 'taken out of your hands.' It's as much under your control now as it's ever been, and if you want to impress me, you have your chance—sort the whole mess out in a way that gets Chester off the hook! And, come to think of it, that saves these poor devils you've had fetched from the past from being treated indefinitely as some kind of—of walking curio!"

"You make it sound too damned easy," Harold countered bitterly. "It's not my fault that Chester lost his temper and killed Joshua, is it? Joshua himself had a good deal to do with it, *I* think."

"Did Joshua have any choice about what happened to him?" Sarah snapped. "Did you consult him before listing him among the—what was the word they've been using?—the 'subjects'?"

"Damn it, how could I have?"

"Exactly. And did you ask Chester how he felt about his invention being used to bring back someone who made a fortune out of buying and selling Negroes?"

"I didn't know about that! Flannagan said he got it from the sugar trade!"

"So did you look up the sugar trade and find out what it was that went the other way in return for sugar cargoes?"

"Of course, I didn't! I—"

"There's no *of course* about it," Sarah rapped. "I'm telling you straight: you want a way to impress me, you just start thinking for yourself instead of letting your staff do the job for you."

"Oh, shut up!" Harold muttered. "I'm going to bed. Jesus, it's four o'clock already and I'm far too tired to argue. Good *night!*"

The room was dreadfully empty when he had stormed away. Sarah stood where she had been earlier, blankly gazing at the inflatable buildings in the distance, which now were limp like cast snakeskins; the lights shining on them were being doused in groups of half a dozen at a time.

It felt as though a world were ending.

While she was still standing miserably contemplating the last traces of the grand reunion party Harold had set such store by, the phone buzzed, and she hurried to answer it before the automatics decided there was no one left in the living zone and switched the call to Harold's bedside.

Pale and tense, Miriam's face appeared in the screen as she put down the switch. "Ah, thank goodness it's you, Sarah!" she exclaimed. "I meant to call you long ago, but we only just got back to New York and this is the first chance I've had to sneak away where Solomon won't hear me talking. Look, this killing at your party—"

"What about it?"

"You know someone handed Dr Waley a sword?"

"Yes, Edgar's. It was the only other one in the whole place; we'd persuaded Sieur Bohun and Sir Godwin to go without because it wasn't until much later than their day that it became the badge of a gentleman to bear arms all the time." Sarah shuddered as she pictured in memory Edgar's impatient discarding of the weapon that was getting in his way as they danced the elegant formal measures of the galliard and the coranto.

"Well, it was a man called Cy Detrick. Solomon smuggled him out. He's apparently been on the Four-S payroll for years. And Solomon is so delighted with what he did tonight, he's hiring him, he's guaranteeing him against your suit for breach of contract because he was supposed to stay with you until the end of this year, and—and I can't stand him! He's such a nasty person he makes my skin crawl. So I want to know: who can I shop him to as an accessory before the fact of culpable homicide?"

There was something so feral about Miriam's expression as she uttered the ridiculously prim and legalistic question that Sarah felt a shiver run down her spine. She said faintly, "Well, it was Detective Commander Helnick of—"

"Get away from that phone!" barked Solomon's voice from the speaker, and a hand like a claw clamped on Miriam's shoulder, dragging her back. She cried out, but Solomon was stronger than she despite being double her age, and in an instant it was his face, thin and crossed with dense dark eyebrows drawn together in a scowl, which occupied the screen before Sarah.

The moment he saw who his wife had been talking to, he reverted to his normal urbane politeness. "My apologies, Sarah," he said softly. "The shock of being present when a murder was committed—I'm afraid it's been too much for Miriam. You understand."

"I understand perfectly about the service Detrick did you," Sarah forced out between clenched teeth.

"Do you? Well, that doesn't bother me—the courts have long recognized industrial espionage as a permissible entry on corporation tax returns, haven't they?"

"I'm not talking about the spying bit. I'm talking about murder!"

"There's nothing to connect me with Detrick's decision to give your Dr Waley a sword, Sarah. Nothing whatever! Good night!"

CHAPTER XIX

"Are you all right, Chester? Are you being treated decently?" Harold demanded from the screen of the phone set into the cell's right-hand wall.

"They don't starve or torture prisoners awaiting trial any longer!" Chester snapped. He was stretched out on the deeply padded and automatically warmed divan bed opposite the screen.

"Did the lawyer I sent for get in touch with you?"

"Nickles? Damn him, yes he did—he turned up about ten minutes after they shoved me in here, and I haven't had any peace since. He only left a moment ago. How about letting me catch some sleep, hm?"

"Please don't be ungrateful," Harold begged. "I'm doing my best for you. I've given orders that adequate time should be made available on Sparky to prepare your defense, and—"

"Sure, sure, I've heard all that," Chester grunted. He sat up on the divan and stared fiercely at Harold's image. "Now you figure this to yourself, will you? I never did anything I regretted less in my entire life than sticking that stinking slave trader in the guts! Hear me? Now cut the circuit and leave me alone!"

"But, you see, Flannagan lied to—"

"Hell, why are you so pleased about offering me Sparky to help my defense? You didn't bother to find out what he could tell you about Joshua, did you? *You* changed your tune very damned fast when your brilliant notion turned sour on you!"

Ebenezer Freitas chewed on the last remaining fragment of his fingernails, tore it loose and spat it out. His stomach was so sour with hunger he was almost faint, and his tongue was like a bad country road in summer; it felt as though, were he to touch it, it would give off clouds of yellow dust.

He had been trying to read the Biblical stories most relevant to his predicament, but he had found his fingers turning up, willy-nilly, the stories of Samson striking water from the ass's jawbone and the children of Israel eating manna in the wilderness.

He was back in the place where he had been penned before. Food had been brought to him, and drink that was so enticing it almost cured the problem of his thirst by making his mouth water. But he was afraid to touch it.

And yet . . .

He stared, puzzled, at the close-printed words of the Bible before him. Memory assured him that this was indeed the same Holy Writ he had studied assiduously all his life.

Could it—*could* it—be true that this ungodly generation was telling the truth? Could the door of time really have been unlocked?

He stared at the three-vee set which he had not touched since he was shown how to operate it. He thought for a long time. Eventually his hand stole out, shaking, and pressed down the switch which lit the screen.

For a long time after, he concentrated on the events and information which it presented to him, until he found himself growing dizzy with the struggle to absorb all he was being told. Then, almost absentmindedly, he realized he had sipped at the drink waiting in a mug close at hand. It tasted like honest milk. He sipped a little more and went on watching.

He was fascinated.

Also he was beginning to be ashamed.

"Mr Freitas is busy, I'm afraid," Helen Whymore told Sarah. "He's been in continuous conference with Louisa since he arrived this morning, apart from ten minutes he spent talking to Jabez Nickles, the lawyer he assigned to help Chester Waley. How is Chester, by the way?"

"I called up before I came over here," Sarah said. "He's asleep. I didn't want to disturb him."

"It's an awful thing to have happen, isn't it?" Helen muttered. "Jimmy Quentin was in here earlier, practically crying. Said the rest of the Timescoop research team were threatening to strike unless he's cleared at the preliminary hearing. They've all offered to donate half their salaries for the current month to the defense fund if it's needed."

"That's nice of them," Sarah said, sighing. "But these days the idea of one man actually killing another—it's going to be the craziest case in history, isn't it?"

"Well, like they say, nothing can set a precedent until it happens for the first time," Helen muttered. "Anyway: can I do anything for you? I have problems in a pile yea high, I'm afraid."

"Yes, of course you have. I don't imagine the ancestors are taking kindly to being penned up again when they must have thought they were about to be let out into the big world for a change."

"You can say that again! The Earl of Winchelsea is the worst, though one of my junior staff had an inspiration and we're piping him some hard-core porn to keep him amused. But Sieur Bohun has found out that there's practically nothing left in the way of wide-open spaces, and he's gone into a sulk because he wanted to get back to hawking and boar hunting, and of course, Sir Godwin is still trying to recruit for his new crusade—*that's* a one-track mind!—and General Wallington, who met Tabitha last night and took a fancy to her probably because she's the only half-way attractive woman who ever looked at him twice, has been threatening writs of habeas corpus if we don't turn her loose immediately and—damn it, why should I bore you with the whole list? It's far too long!"

"Does it include Edgar?"

"Him? No, he's been a perfect lamb, and the only calls we've had about him this morning so far have been either more proposals of marriage—they've come from as far away as Ganymede now—or else invitations for him to take up jobs as a dancing instructor. Now, on the other hand, the Hemisphere Civil Liberties Union has been warning us that we as a corporation are liable as accessories before the fact of incitement to racial discrimination because of what Joshua said, and—hell, sorry. I didn't mean to run off at the mouth simply because you haven't heard it all already."

"What's this done to the general public image of Freitas Interplanetary?"

"Knocked the bottom out of it, I believe." Helen sighed. "Louisa deals with all that kind of thing, of course, but I did ask her about it the only chance I got this morning, when Mr Freitas called down to say he wanted us to try and figure out a way of getting the ancestors out of their quarters and into the modern world. And then Louisa, who was in the same circuit, said something about losing thirty points."

Sarah whistled. "Lord! Well, keep on with it, won't you? It isn't fair for them to be cooped up here like"—she consciously borrowed Harold's phrase—"animals. We're going to have to return them to the world sooner or later. Meantime, would anyone mind my dropping in on Edgar?"

"Well, strictly the police did say—oh, damn the police! Edgar's not only just about the brightest but also the most adaptable of the whole bunch. Carry on. I won't say a word."

Sighing over the fantastic spectacles which his three-vee screen showed him, yet resigned to waiting until the people of this new and astonishing day were ready to let him go out and enjoy them in reality, Edgar glanced up as the door of his room clicked. Delight overcame him as he realized his visitor was Sarah; an instant later, his pleasure gave way to dismay as he read the unhappy expression on her face.

"My lady—Sarah, I mean—what is amiss, if I may ask?"

Dropping into a chair after giving him a perfunctory peck on the cheek, she shrugged. "Nothing you can do anything about, I'm afraid. You know about the killing which took place at last night's party?"

"Yes, I asked about it, and after some persuasion I found one to explain it to me. But what is so terrible? Did not the Indian—?" Edgar checked himself. "Forgive me; when I first saw the man with dark skin whom they call Dr Chester I assumed he must be one of the New World Indians, and I still have not forgotten my former error. He is, is he not, a blackamoor whose forefathers were rudely snatched from their home in Africa?"

"That's right."

"Well—" Edgar hesitated. "Did he not behave as any man of spirit should, learning that this Joshua whom he slew had been the thief who profited by this trade in human flesh?"

"I'm afraid we don't accept that kind of behavior any longer, Edgar," Sarah said. "I'm very much afraid for him. Still, never mind—he has an excellent lawyer to argue in his defense, and Harold has promised unlimited money to support him. It's you who are worrying me; I can't do anything for Chester right now."

"I?" Alarmed, Edgar clapped his hand to his chest. "Why should it be I who disturb you?"

"Oh, I don't mean you specifically." Sarah made a vague depressed gesture. "Edgar, does it come as a surprise to you to learn that in 2066 people can still be out and out *stupid?*"

Edgar tried and failed to control a grin. He said, "Not in the least. So far, what little I have seen suggests that men have remained men, much as they were in my day—capable of getting angry, or drunken, or weary. You have new skills, but it is not my impression that you have more skills, each for each."

"You're a very wise boy," Sarah said, and hastily corrected herself. "Forgive me: I shouldn't have said 'boy'."

"Am I not?" Edgar countered. "Compared with Sieur Bohun, who was born in the year one thousand and something?"

Sarah threw her fair head back and laughed outright. It was something which, during the night, she might have believed she could never look forward to again. She said, "Then what does that make me—a baby, surely?"

"I can hardly think of you as anything but a most lovely and kind mistress," Edgar said.

"Thank you. Thank you very much." But a cloud passed across Sarah's face as she spoke. "Oh!" she added, "I wish I could do something to fix this damned problem we're facing! You know you're going to be locked up here until the police are satisfied none of the rest of you is liable to do what Joshua did?"

Edgar looked alarmed. "But it would be terrible to be prisoned, with the wonders of the—the *twenty-first* century behind that magic window in the three-vee set and know that one might never venture forth among them! Surely, with all the variety and richness of your world, you can find some place for each and all of us?"

Sarah sat bolt upright. "Say that again!" she requested, and immediately countermanded herself. "No, never mind —I heard you clearly. You're damned right! Why didn't *I* think of that?"

Excitedly she jumped to her feet and threw her arms around him. "You're a genius!" she exclaimed. "If I can cure one of the two problems facing us, that'll do more than halve the total! Bless you, Edgar, and excuse me for having to dash off. But I think you've just—what's the old phrase?—cut the Gordian knot!"

"I'd rather unloose the girdle of Venus," Edgar said hopefully.

"Edgar, you're a darling and I'm terribly flattered, but when you get out of here, you're going to find the girls sort of lying down in front of you and waving their legs in the air and you'll be able to take your pick and it won't be any more than you deserve."

She gave him a final smacking kiss on the cheek and dashed for the door.

CHAPTER XX

"Mr Nickles, good afternoon to you. Won't you sit down?" Flannagan, the genealogist, waved at a chair as the lawyer entered his office, furnished with valuable antiques and decorated with heraldic escutcheons and portraits of satisfied clients.

Nickles nodded his thanks, took the chair, and glanced curiously at a lit phone-screen on the wall which displayed the face of a rather worried-looking young woman.

"Ah—do you know Mrs Nell Charters?" Flannagan murmured. "In view of the nature of your business, I felt it best to have my own counsel sit in on this discussion."

"Ah!" Nickles snapped his fingers. "Yes, of course, we have met, I remember now. You're on the staff of Schatzenheim Solar System Services, aren't you, Mrs Charters?"

"I used to be. I'm in independent practice now but I still handle occasional business for the corporation when I'm invited to."

"Hmm—I see. Well, no doubt you're fully aware why it is I've come to call on you, Mr Flannagan? Perhaps I'm a trifle conservative, but I always feel that, in a delicate situation such as the present one, it's better to make face-to-face contact than to talk by way of a phone link. Even a sealed line, after all, doesn't give quite the sense of security and the ability to talk freely which one experiences in the total privacy of a closed room of proper modern construction."

Excellent. Flannagan's response was to shoot an agonized glance at Mrs Charters as though to say: *Why didn't you mention that point to me?*

"However, each to his own tastes," Nickles continued. "I don't want to take up any more of your valuable time than is strictly necessary, so suppose we get down to brass tacks at once, shall we? You do realize, no doubt, that it was as the result of the information furnished by yourself that Mr Harold Freitas selected the nine—ah—ancestors he brought together at his recent reunion party, with such disastrous consequences?"

"Mr Nickles," Flannagan said fervently, "believe me, if I'd had the least inkling of what he was planning to do—"

"Mr Nickles!" Mrs Charters cut in. "May I remind you of the ancient platitude that in law a man can only be held responsible for the foreseeable consequences of his acts? Something which Freitas Interplanetary was keeping under an ultra-strict security blanket is by definition not foreseeable."

"Ah, yes. But, you see, an announcement was made on January first concerning the planned reunion, and it didn't take place until the sixth, did it? Being aware that he had —shall we say?—*weighted* the information he had supplied to Mr Freitas, I believe it was his duty as a citizen for Mr Flannagan to get in touch with his client and make clear the omissions and reservations he had previously no doubt chosen to make in order to spare the feelings of Mr Freitas. In particular, when he was contacted by Cyrus Detrick, who—"

"But the bastard came to me posing as a regular client himself!" Flannagan burst out. "How was I to know that his interest in the Freitas reunion was any more than the ordinary curiosity which everyone was feeling as a result of the news they'd just heard? What's more natural than to ask a genealogist questions about such a subject?"

"That's for the court computer to decide," Nickles said briskly. "And court computers are very, very logical indeed. Would you not agree, Mrs Charters, that it's been one of the great twenty-first-century breakthroughs in jurisprudence—the introduction of computers to evaluate evidence?"

Mrs Charters said nothing. But she looked daggers at him.

"Helen, can I use a corner of your office for a minute?" Sarah exclaimed, dashing into the room. "There's something I want to ask Sparky—very urgently."

"Why, by all means," Helen said. "But please keep it quiet, hm?"

"Yes, of course."

"You know the codes and everything?"

"I think so." Dropping into a chair facing the spare communications panel, Sarah punched keys on the board under the screen. Instantly the familiar Voltaire mask appeared. "Yes, that's fine. You carry on with what you're doing and I'll try not to disturb you. Sparky, Sarah Freitas here. Look, about all these ancestors of Harold's—you know we're being pestered from the police side to keep them securely penned up in case another of them does what Joshua did, and from the Civil Liberties side to turn them loose right away?"

"Yes, Mrs Freitas, I've been fully briefed on the recent developments in that area."

"Well, what I want to know—" Sarah drew a deep breath. The question she was about to put seemed so obvious she was half afraid of making a fool of herself, but that was a risk she had to take. She started again.

"What I want to know is . . ."

Most of the day Harold spent in his office with his head buried in his hands, except when he was interrupted by a call from one of his staff. Outside calls—from news agencies and other pests—were being filtered and only personal or official ones reached him. His head kept ringing with Sarah's words after the party, to the effect that if he wanted to impress her he needed to start doing his own thinking instead of leaving it to his subordinates.

Yet thinking seemed to be out of the question. All he could bring to mind was the ghastly truth of her charge that he had treated his ancestors as "presents to himself." He had been brought up to be very proud of this forefathers; now, with earthquake violence, pride had turned to shame. To think, for example, that a Freitas had engaged in the slave trade!

What other dreadful scandals were lurking in the background? Luckily, the climate of opinion had changed enough for something like the Earl of Winchelsea's pederasty not to create a major furore except among the most conservative and reactionary groups, but according to Louisa, today had already seen some thirty points chopped off the favorable public rating for Freitas

Interplanetary, and so far only the killing itself had been publicized.

Or—was that all? It was more than three hours since he had brought himself to punch for a newsfax sheet. He stirred from his brown study, bracing himself for a shock, and ordered one. As its limp tongue spilled from the printer he saw bold, ugly headlines, and his heart sank.

This was terrible! Where had they got all these scraps of dirt from? Flannagan? Hardly—the moment he thought of it, he'd sent Nickles around to the genealogist's office to put the fear of God into him and ensure his mouth stayed shut until after Chester's trial, at least. But it couldn't very well be Detrick, could it?

Yes, it could be. The realization made his mouth go sour. To be more precise, it could be someone who got at Detrick—and that meant Solomon Schatzenheim, green with envy at the trick which had been put over on him.

Well, regardless of who had been responsible, the beans had been spilled by the cartload. Here were separate and detailed data on each of the ancestors: here was the story of Horatio shooting poor Mr Robbins; here was an account—culled, by the look of it, from a contemporary source—of Tabitha's famous White House reception; here was an excerpt from testimony recorded at a Salem witch trial.

He couldn't go on. It was too dreadful. He groaned and threw the fax sheet aside.

At long last he was having to admit to himself that all his motives in organizing this reunion of his ancestors and relatives had been unworthy ones. Chester had been wholly justified in saying that he had reduced a significant research breakthrough to the status of a toy. His cheeks burned as he thought of all the other faults he could be accused of—vanity, self-importance, greed, the desire to outface Solomon Schatzenheim and the reflected glory he enjoyed from his own grand family reunion.

He took a deep breath and sat up straight in his chair. Just to top everything off, he was now openly being referred to as a slave owner himself, given that the ancestors he had fetched out of the past had never had the chance to say whether or not they wanted to undergo this terrifying experience! A guarded, but nonetheless pointed, expression of this view had caught his eye on a bit of the crumpled newsfax sheet he had tossed aside.

Blazes, that was too much! He was going to get out from under this by hook or by crook—*somehow* he was going to get out from under!

He punched for Sparky with determined fingers.

"Miriam?" Solomon said as he strode into the apartment and, receiving no reply, repeated louder: "Miri-a-am!"

Still there was no answer. Standing uncertainly in the middle of the living zone, he glanced around. There was a flag up on the phone to signify that a message for him had been recorded during his absence. He went over and flipped it down; at once Miriam's voice rang out from the speaker, though the screen remained blank.

"I finally got what I wanted," she said sweetly. "Last night you bruised my shoulder when you forced me away from the phone while I was talking to Sarah Freitas. I had that conversation recorded, and the tape went to my lawyers first thing after they opened for business today. They advise me it constitutes *prima facie* proof of physical cruelty. Furthermore, they inform me that, in the event of your conviction for withholding relevant evidence concerning the likelihood of a breach of the peace at the Freitas reunion party, I myself might well face an accessory charge if I continue to associate with you. So I'm leaving, and I'm not sorry. Also, by the way, this is a self-destructive recording, so unless you thought of rerecording it on your own equipment, you can forget about my admission that I wanted to provoke you into hitting me, or something. Goodbye, Solomon; I hope you're happier with your next wife."

Solomon roared in wordless fury, but there was a wisp of smoke winding up from the speaker to show what she claimed was true: the recording was destroying itself as it was played.

The triumph he had felt at sabotaging Freitas's reunion evaporated along with the recording tape.

Harold drew a deep breath, his mind miraculously cleared of the clouds that had darkened it all day. It was so obvious once one had seen the point! Instead of being ashamed at his own vanity, he was now ashamed of his own blindness.

He cut the connection with Sparky and rapped out the call-code for Jabez Nickles instead. When the lawyer appeared in the screen, he barked, "Mr Nickles! What happens if a court computer at a major trial finds itself trapped in a logical paradox?"

Nickles blinked at him. "Well—well, I'm not really sure. The problem has never arisen. But I doubt very much whether the trial would be postponed or started again from scratch—the defense would have too many valid pleas to enter concerning inordinate cruelty, excessive suspense and so forth. Why?"

"Because that's what's going to happen when they arraign Chester Waley. Listen carefully!"

"By the way, Mrs Freitas," Sparky said as she thanked him and made to cut the circuit, "during our discussion, I've also been interrogated by Mr Freitas on related subjects. I think I should inform you that I've passed on to him the same answers to the same questions as you yourself have put."

"Good lord!" Sarah said, staring at the Voltaire mask. "You mean Harold got to the conclusion as I did, all by himself? The so-and-so! Just when I was expecting to . . ." The words trailed away, and she suddenly smiled. "No, it's much better this way, come to think of it. But thanks for letting me know, Sparky. Thanks very much indeed."

CHAPTER XXI

"I've got it!" Harold announced jubilantly as he marched across the living zone of the LA penthouse toward the lounge where Sarah was sitting, sipping at a tall frosted glass. He brushed aside the hand she held it with and gave her a smacking kiss, which she returned with interest and enthusiasm.

"Well, you've certainly got something!" she said when she had extricated herself again. "I thought you'd given up doing that when you took over Freitas Interplanetary—decided it was beneath your dignity or something!"

He gave her a mock scowl which turned into a grin. "Cast your eyes over this," he said, tossing a folded document into her lap, and turned toward the liquor console. "I think it explains itself, but if there's anything which isn't clear, just ask me."

Sarah unfolded the paper and glanced down it. As she had expected, it consisted of a list of the names of the nine ancestors, together with a series of other names underneath each and various explanatory footnotes. Taking advantage of Harold's back's being turned, she smiled covertly. Well, he had at least solved the problem at the same time as she had, which meant he was catching up for a change.

Realizing that he was on his way to rejoin her, she put on a more innocent expression.

"Ah—do I understand this properly?" she said. "Is it ideas for places where your ancestors can fit into our modern society without the risk of anything else happening like with Joshua and Chester?"

"Precisely. But it goes beyond that: the people listed there are ones that Sparky says we can persuade to act as bailees and guarantors for my ancestors. According to Nickles, Detective Commander Helnick must show cause for his injunction concerning them within forty-eight hours of the application, which means he's going to have to convince a judge tomorrow—or rather, he's going to have to convince the court computer the judge consults. If you turn right through to the end of the list, you'll see that Sparky suggests you make one or two of the initial approaches. Would you mind doing that for me?"

Sarah flipped to the back of the multipage document and pretended to ponder, though she already knew what her answer would be. She said in a musing tone, "It's a shame we can't sort out Chester's trouble as easily. Have you seen him today?"

"Not in person, but I called him at the jail and Nickles went to see him first thing, of course. But don't you worry about him too much, will you?"

Sarah looked up in horror. "Harold, what an awful thing to say!"

"I mean it," Harold said, plumping himself down close by her side. "At the moment, Chester is getting a kind of inverted enjoyment out of what's happened; apparently we can expect it to last for another night before he really begins to get frustrated and miserable. I mean, it's not everyone who has the chance to get back directly at someone who's done the worst kind of dirt to his ancestors, is it?"

"Well, I admit that if I'd been in Chester's place I'd have kicked Joshua's ass for him, woman or not," Sarah said tartly. "But that's a far cry from a homicide charge."

"What homicide charge?" Harold said smugly, and waited to see if she would catch on.

"Who?" demanded Adelina Freitas-Lockerby-Horn, Grand Crested Cockatoo of the Sisters of the Southern Order of Neo-Chivalry. And, as the automatics dutifully repeated the information they had just given her, her mind worked frantically.

On the one hand, of course, the way things were at the moment . . .

But on the other, naturally, if there were the least chance of . . .

"Ask her to wait one second," she requested, and snatched a glance at herself in a nearby mirror. A touch or two was all she required to perfect her appearance; then she slid into a chair facing the phone and cooed into the mikes.

"Why, Cousin Sarah! I may call you Sarah, may I not, even on the strength of our brief acquaintance since the party you held the other night? I can't begin to tell you how distressed I was, we all were, to learn what had transpired. But then, of course, those were hotter-blooded days than our own tame era, were they not? And lacking the experience which we moderns have in the correct way to deal with those of our brethren who suffer the misfortune of darker epidermises and the concomitant characteristics—"

At the other end, Sarah had to grit her teeth to stop herself shouting that Chester Waley was probably going to collect a Nobel for his work on the Timescoop. But she retained her composure just sufficiently to be able to go ahead with the wheedling speech Sparky had drafted for her, and in minutes she had Mrs Freitas-Lockerby-Horn practically shaking with combined anger and excitement.

"Of course, of course! It sounds like the least any decent person could do," she declared. "And, of course, it will be such a boost, such a marvelous inspiration for us all in these apathetic days! Just let me know how I can implement the suggestion."

Chief Rocket Bomb composed himself before the phone, arranging his magnificent synthetic buffalo robe into the correct folds, crossed his legs and with one toe touched the switch. Raising his hand in greeting, he said solemnly, "How!"

Harold echoed him, the while gazing doubtfully at the polychrome decorations which cross-hatched the Chief's forehead, cheeks and chin. There seemed to be an awful gulf to bridge in both space and time, but one of the things Sparky had been most thoroughly programmed with was cultural-analysis material, and if he said this was the thing to do, this was the thing to do.

He cleared his throat and launched into the conversational exposition the computer had prepared for him. He saw a gleam appear in the Chief's eyes almost at once, but of course protocol demanded that he take a long, slow, roundabout route to an affirmative.

But he'd get there, eventually.

A round-faced, rather simpering woman of late middle age appeared in Sarah's screen before a complex three-dimensional montage of famous eighteenth-century documents and portraits: all the signatories of the Declaration of Independence, for instance, encircling the Declaration itself reproduced on imitation parchment.

"Why, Mrs Freitas—what a pleasure to speak with the bearer of a name so honored in our nation's history! And what can I do for you?"

Sarah told her.

"General Wallington!" Harold said in a hearty man-to-man tone. "I think you're by far the most appropriate person to consult regarding a certain rather delicate matter which has cropped up. Of course, I suppose I really have no business mentioning this, but someone who carries through as many government contracts as I do, with my company, inevitably hears the occasional whisper on the grapevine, so I think I'm correct in saying, am I not, that your duties are frequently concerned with intelligence training? No, please"—raising a hand—"I'm asking you neither to confirm nor to deny that assertion, simply to listen to me for a moment and let me know what you think about . . ."

"The First Secretary, please," Sarah said when she had her connection with the British Embassy in Washington. And, after a moment: "I'm so sorry to disturb you, but I can't think of anyone who's in a better position to do something to right a scandalous injustice. At least, that's what I think it is, and it's due to nothing more than the inertia of the law this side of the Atlantic. It does so often happen, doesn't it, that the law falls behind the events of real life! That's where you're so fortunate in Britain, not having the ideals of an earlier day fossilized into a written constitution and the rest of it."

She saw the Englishman preening with reflected glory, and knew she was over the first hurdle. Good old Sparky!

Ishmael ibn-Abdallah hastily checked the special controls he had had fitted to his phone to make sure that the image from his end would go out with the maximum possible loading toward the black. He was, in fact, a rather pale shade of café au lait and could never deepen it significantly regardless of how long he spent under ultraviolet lamps every day. But, of course, it wasn't fitting for someone in his position in the New Reformed Orthodox Mosque of Genuine Islam, Incorporated, to present any paler an image than he could possibly help.

Satisfied that he would appear on the screen at the other end as a near-ebony figure, he pressed the switch and snapped, "Well, Freitas? What do you want—to try and get out from under the load of guilt your unlamented slaver-ancestor left you with? There's no getting away with it that easily." He glowered sternly at the white man in the phone.

Swallowing his pride in accordance with Sparky's recommendation, Harold uttered soothing words of agreement and casually let fall during them the clue which, the computer promised, would fester in ibn-Abdallah's mind like a poisoned barb until he caught on to what he was being offered.

"Count Alfonso," Sarah said meekly, "I called up to tell you how much I regretted not being able to give you the opportunity you requested to talk with Sieur Bohun the other night. It's a terrible shame that your interest is so concentrated on him, because, of course, the question of astral influences is of such concern to someone else among the group, but, of course—"

Count Alfonso leaned forward against the background of crossed Toledo swords and astrological charts in his Harpalus home; not being used to the second-and-a-half delay in the Lunar circuit, Sarah had talked past the correct point. But it didn't matter. His eyes were gleaming in just the way one might expect from someone who had emigrated to the Moon in order to make more perfect observations of the planetary influences beyond the atmosphere of Earth.

"And that," Harold said pointedly, "leaves Edgar."

There was a moment of silence between them. At length, Sarah sighed and leaned back in her chair. She said, "Harold dear, whatever else you may be, you're certainly no fool, are you?"

"I hope not. Except, perhaps, where you're concerned." He looked extremely depressed.

Reaching to take his hand, she gave him a wan smile. "I'm sorry. It's me who's been silly, isn't it? You—ah—you do know what I'm talking about, don't you?"

Harold nodded. "And I didn't have to consult Sparky to catch on," he added.

"No, I didn't suppose you'd need to." Sarah jumped up and walked across to the window wall, with its magnificent panorama of the high pale towers of Greater Los Angeles. Over her shoulder she said, "Well, it *was* a silly thing for me to do—a bit of prime self-deception. I—" She licked her lips. "I took a look at the psychoportrait of Edgar that Sparky raised, along with all the others. No one else seems to have been very interested so far because he's been so amenable and untroublesome. But you know what it says?"

"More or less. He doesn't care about women, you or anyone else. Not yet. He's far too young. In spite of having been made to behave like a man because of social circumstances in his day, his real enthusiasm is a sort of childlike wonder at the marvels of new places and new spectacles. To him, this continent is genuinely the New World. He's never even set foot in a foreign country before!"

"And there are lots and lots and lots of really new worlds waiting for him," Sarah murmured. "The Moon, Mars, Ganymede."

She briskened. "Well, at least, right to the end, he does remain the one who's caused us the fewest difficulties."

CHAPTER XXII

Promptly at eleven A.M. local time, Judge Valentine Bushmill took his place on the bench in the State Capitol's main courtroom. By rights, a simple case like this, involving no more than showing cause for an injunction to restrain certain persons from disturbing the planetary peace, ought to have been heard in some small out-of-the-way court elsewhere in the building or even elsewhere in the state.

However, such was the interest this whole affair had aroused that from five or six o'clock in the morning people had been lining up for admission to the public gallery—actually physically waiting, in the chill of early morning, when they could have stayed home and watched over the three-vee. In fact, hardly any of them had succeeded in getting into the court, he noticed as he grumpily surveyed it. There had been some hurried rearrangements made: the legal personnel had overflowed into the press section, the press section had overflowed into the public seats—which were a tangle of cameras, mikes, mixing gear and portable computerized law commentators—and that minute handful of the actual public which had managed to squeeze in was confined to notable personalities who had doubtless exercised special influence. Right at the back, for instance, he noticed Solomon Schatzenheim, glowering as though he'd just been given a hotfoot and failed to catch the culprit. What in the Solar System was he spending the day here for, instead of in the New York headquarters of his financial empire?

Somehow, the Judge decided as he stared at the unprecedented number of attorneys and counselors who crowded into the space before him, he was getting the impression that he wasn't going to enjoy this case.

But at least, if it developed into ridiculous complications, he wouldn't have to rely solely on his own mental faculties as he might have had to in his grandfather's day. At least he had the services of one of the ultramodern legal computers which had recently so revolutionized litigation that appeals were very nearly a thing of the past. Verdicts handed down with their assistance were like judgments of Solomon; they carried prestige, cachet, and, above all, some greater semblance of justice than ever before in history.

He glanced down at the unwinking bank of lights on his chair arm and drew faint comfort from the realization that they were working perfectly. He cleared his throat and looked up again.

"The clerk will read the process that we are to try," he said.

The clerk did so, at length. Boiled down, what he was saying was that there had been a major felony committed, to wit a culpable homicide, and the police were seeking an injunction to restrain certain persons named in an adjoined list from mingling with the public for fear of a repetition.

"I see." Judge Bushmill nodded. So did the computer—or at least the correct lights had flickered beside him. "Who's asking for the injunction—you, Detective Commander?" He cocked an eyebrow at Helnick, whom he knew well, and received a nod of affirmation.

"Then what is this—ah—galaxy of legal talent before my chair?" the Judge demanded.

The man on the end of the line of counselors rose. "I'm Jabez Nickles, your honor," he said. "I wish your honor's permission to appear as an *amicus curiae* representing the interests of Harold Freitas III and Freitas Interplanetary Corporation."

Fair enough. The Judge nodded. He'd been expecting that, since the Freitases were so intimately involved in the case, but that left—one, two, three—heavens above, that left *eight* more lawyers in the line! He asked the next one to account for himself.

"Lionel X. Donkin, your honor. *Amicus curiae*, with your honor's consent. Representing the interests of Miss Tabitha Freitas and the Hemisphere Joint Services Intelligence Agency."

"I *beg* your pardon?" the Judge said, blinking. "What in the world have they got to do with this case?"

"I think that will become adequately clear to your

honor as the hearing progresses," Donkin said suavely.

"I hope so! And you?" The Judge pointed to his neighbor.

Rising, the lawyer said, "P.V. Macgillícuddy, your honor, likewise *amicus curiae*, representing the interests of the Earl of Winchelsea and Poitenne and the Daughters of the American Revolution."

"What?" The Judge's eyes bulged. By now the incongruity of the shared interests which the lawyers claimed to be looking after was becoming apparent to the reporters and public at the back of the courtroom, and there was a buzz of excited discussion. He quelled it with a glare and turned to the next lawyer in line, a tall man with a feather in his hair.

"Brave Speaker-with-Forked-Tongue, your honor," he said. "Also friend of court. Noble tribe of Seshawawa Indians. Sieur Bohun de Freitas." He sat down, not being a man to waste words.

"Oh, my goodness," the Judge muttered under his breath. But so far the computer was indicating that everything was in order. Mutely he pointed to the next lawyer again.

"I'm Sir Mortimer Bellamy-Francis, KC, your honor," this one said. He wore the powdered white wig and long black robes of his office, improbably out of place in the ultramodern American court but logical enough, considering the Freitases' British connections. "Also seeking the privilege of being concerned as an *amicus curiae*, on behalf of Sir Godwin de Freitas-Molyneux and the British Crown."

That provoked a positive storm of comment, and the Judge had to punch for a siren to be sounded in order to drown it out.

"One more such outburst, and I'll clear the court!" he warned sternly. "Mr—I mean Sir Mortimer: what has the British Crown to do with the case before me?"

"Like me learned colleague, your honor," Sir Mortimer said with a sketch for a bow, "I believe that will become clear as the hearing proceeds."

"I certainly hope so," the Judge grunted. "Well, how about you?"

They were all *amici curiae*. The remainder of them turned out to be Reverend Counselor Donald Sebastian, representing Ebenezer Freitas and the Combined Methodist, Episcopalian, Congregationalist, Baptist and Unitarian Churches of North America; Licensed Pleader in the Cause of Justice Achmed Salah, representing Buffalo Hank Freitas and the New Reformed Orthodox Mosque of Genuine Islam, Inc.; and Abogado Don Felipe O'Shaughnessy, representing Horatio Freitas and the Pan-Solar League of Believers in the Influence of Unseen Forces, a well-known crank group with adherents among some of the highest society in the Solar System.

Groaning, the Judge asked the computer for a rough count of the people whose interests were being looked after by this string of lawyers, and instantly a figure flicked up on the miniaturized screen before him: "Appx. 200,000,000."

That must set some kind of record, the Judge reflected sadly. Still, throughout the foregoing, Detective Commander Helnick had sat quite impassively, as though he at least had been expecting something of this kind. That was reassuring.

"Very well," he sighed. "I'll direct that you all be entered on the record as friends of the court and permit you to act as such during the hearing. But I warn you: I am maintaining strict computerized control over the relevance of questions not put by the attorneys-in-chief, and I shall come down very hard on anyone who abuses the privilege I'm according you. Well, Detective Commander, would you take the stand, please?"

Expressionless as ever, the policeman complied.

"What's Freitas trying to get away with this time?" Solomon Schatzenheim fumed to Mrs Charters, seated next to him. The overcrowding and the heat in the courtroom were uncivilized, and he was getting fretful.

"As far as I can see," she whispered back, "he's simply trying to confuse the issue. Jabez Nickles is a tricky character. I don't see how it can possibly be more than that. But I must admit I never expected him to rope in anything like the forces he's mustered: the Joint Services Intelligence Agency, the British government, the church . . ."

She shook her head, looking miserable.

In impeccable style, Helnick described the grounds for the injunction he was seeking, recounting that a brawl or affray had taken place during the Freitas family reunion at the Grand Canyon; that he had been sent for when someone died in consequence of a sword blow; that the forensic findings confirmed the story that a person from a previous age had picked a quarrel unjustifiably; that such historical persons could not be expected to behave as civilized modern people did—and so on. In general, he built up a neat and tidy argument in favor of granting his request.

In the seats reassigned to the press, reporters shrugged and leaned back. It sounded like a foregone conclusion now. At most, the Freitases had secured a slight delay, but from today on, according to the portable legal commentators they had brought with them, they could only hope for a drawn-out series of hearings to determine whether it was permissible for human beings to be confined as the police demanded.

At the conclusion of Helnick's testimony, the Judge surreptitiously punched for a probability evaluation of the success of the application he was supposed to adjudicate. The computer quoted a figure in the high nineties, about as high a reading as he had ever seen.

Unable, however, to convince himself that Nickles might not have some dastardly trick up his sleeve, he glanced at the Freitases' lawyer and invited him to cross-examine.

"We concede this witness's evidence," Nickles said, half-rising. "No questions, thank you."

Instantly the computer's screen clicked to the highest reading it was capable of: 99.99 percent. The Judge almost gasped aloud.

"Next witness," he said faintly.

So the various prosecution witnesses traipsed across the stand, and as they came and went, the Judge finally caught on to what was happening. He cursed himself for his own stupidity. Of course! This was one of the oldest tricks in the book.

Faced with a killing at a gathering of some of the world's richest and most famous personalities, Helnick had decided that he wasn't going to risk losing a conviction by smart legal maneuvering on the part of his wealthy opponents. He had applied for this injunction not because he genuinely believed that these—these ancestors of the Freitas family would be dangerous if allowed to roam at large, but because he wanted to play through the entire evidence on which his case depended in a context where Chester Waley's status as a research scientist and other mitigatory points could not be considered relevant.

It was shameful! It was unfair! The Judge almost said so. But those four nines still glared up at him, and he held his tongue.

"Does that complete the case for the police?" he half-whispered. Why in the world hadn't that fool Nickles made any use of the forces he had mustered? He'd assembled legal talent enough to make a regular court computer run in circles chasing its own tail! "It does? Very well, Mr Nickles: it's for you now to show cause why the injunction should not be granted."

Nickles rose with a musing expression. He said, "May it please the court, I'd like to start by addressing my remarks directly to the court computer."

"Er—yes, very well." The Judge activated the necessary circuits.

"You are recognized, Counselor Nickles," the computer said with built-in formality. "Kindly proceed!"

Nickles glanced up into nowhere, his manner abstracted. "Ah—before doing that, I'd like to confirm that all the details of the prosecution's case have been properly recorded and comprehended by the computer advising the Judge. For example, I'd like the computer to tell me relevant biographical details concerning the person alleged to have been killed at the Grand Canyon party we've been hearing about. That is, Joshua William Freitas."

"Joshua William Freitas," the computer said. "Born Liverpool, England, 16th April 1746, married Eliza née Waterbury 12th November 1771, died London, England—

scrrch. Died—SCRRCH! SCRRCH! Fiddle-de-dee, fiddle-de-dum, the fly has eaten the currant bun. *Flooch!* Died London—*ScrrrrCH!*"

Before the Judge's horrified eyes, the little lights flicked wildly on and off, and from beneath the floorboards on which rested his chair there came a distinct smell of burning insulation.

CHAPTER XXIII

"It's working!" whooped Harold joyfully, and threw his arms around Sarah. In the big three-vee screen they could see Nickles adopting an expression of polite surprise, and from the speaker emerged the sound of his solicitous inquiry to the Judge:

"Is anything wrong, your honor?"

Frantically Judge Bushmill punched for reserve circuits to take over, but even as he activated them, they failed in turn. There was a tremendous hubbub in the courtroom now, and in the end he had to use his siren again. As the crowd subsided into silence, he raised his head glumly.

"Mr Nickles, it would appear that you have successfully sabotaged the computer here."

"Your honor!" Nickles said in tones of shocked disparagement. "I merely asked it a perfectly proper question!"

"Yes, I'm sorry," the Judge said with an effort. "But the fact stands: it can't cope with the paradox of having witnesses on oath swear to the death of a man in 2066 in Arizona who has previously been described in affidavits as dying in London, England, in the eighteenth century. Hmmm! I believe this situation is unprecedented; I will entertain motions concerning our course of action."

The prosecuting attorney jumped up. "Your honor, I move that we adjourn until a new computer can be installed that is immune to this cheap underhand trickery!"

Instantly, as one man, lawyers O'Shaughnessy, Salah, Sebastian, Bellamy-Francis, Speaker-with-Forked-Tongue, Macgillicuddy, Donkin and Nickles said, "Objection, your honor. This is a hearing to show cause for an injunction that will deprive our clients of their normal liberties and the law states it must be dealt with within forty-eight hours of the application's being filed."

Someone laughed in the back of the courtroom. The Judge glared in that direction and decided that whoever might have found this amusing, it couldn't have been Solomon Schatzenheim; he was looking like a thundercloud.

"I move," Nickles said, "that the hearing be concluded without computer assistance." He beamed sunnily.

"No," the Judge said. "There are other courts and other computers in this building, and I feel I need the guidance they can offer. Clerk, find us another courtroom; we'll adjourn for thirty minutes while you do so."

"At least the Judge isn't letting himself be browbeaten," Nell Charters told Solomon in a tone of false optimism. "He told Nickles where he could get off, didn't he?"

"He did that because he was scared," Solomon growled. "You can't be much of a lawyer yourself if you didn't realize that. He's afraid Nickles has another ace up his sleeve which he'll need computer help to spot. And to be candid, I'm afraid of that, too."

He relapsed into gloomy silence. Watching from home over the three-vee, Harold and Sarah caught sight of his miserable face and hugged each other with glee.

"Now, Mr Nickles!" Judge Bushmill said, having made doubly certain that this computer was in proper working order. He cast a glance around the new courtroom; it was markedly smaller and consequently far more crowded, and distinguished members of the public who had had seats before were now compelled to stand. Oh, well . . .

"This computer has been instructed to give overriding precedence to the testimony of human witness on oath," he continued. "I am assured by the technicians that this eliminates the risk of paradox breakdown. For example, faced with the contradictory information that Joshua Freitas died in London on one date and in Arizona on another, the computer will now accord priority to the sworn testimony it has received from the witness stand. We cannot allow quibbles to stand in the way of the truth."

"Very good, your honor," Nickles said with a bow. "I am to understand, am I not, that this machine has been fully acquainted with the testimony so far? It knows all about the admitted impalement of Joshua Freitas on a sword held at the time by Dr Chester Waley, and his consequent death at the Freitas reunion party on January sixth?"

"Er—yes," the Judge assured him nervously. Now what was this so-and-so going to pull out of the bag? It would only be fair and right for him to get the better of Helnick in view of the latter's attempt to have Chester Waley tried *in absentia,* but the way he was setting about it was enough to give any judge ulcers.

There was a moment of tense silence, with everyone in the courtroom and uncounted millions of three-vee viewers hanging on the lawyer's next words. Then he raised his head and said loudly and clearly, "I should like to call my first witness now, your honor. Will Joshua William Freitas take the stand?"

The silence suddenly became stunned instead of fascinated. Through the courtroom door, looking very sorry for himself, Joshua Freitas appeared escorted by an usher and everyone watching at once recognized him from the three-vee coverage of the reunion and the subsequent press pictures that had been published.

Underneath Judge Bushmill's chair there was a mechanical shrieking noise, and the newly programmed computer blew up.

Gingerly fingering the plastiskin dressings which had been put over his many small cuts and bruises, Judge Bushmill said hopelessly, "It's no good, Mr Nickles. I'm going to have to finish the hearing without a computer, aren't I?"

"Yes, your honor," Nickles agreed sympathetically. "I guess I might as well admit now that my argument has been entirely planned by Sparky, the Freitas Interplanetary computer, which is capable of resolving fourth-order paradoxes. No judicial computer in this state can cope with better than second-order ones."

Pacing up and down on the other side of the Judge's robing room, the prosecuting attorney gave him a glower.

"I think," Nickles continued, "that in view of the circumstances, the police might consider abandoning their application. Suppose, while they're clearing the rubble from the courtroom, we"—he gestured at his eight colleagues

—"briefly summarize what it is we are suggesting to you, apart from the fundamental issue of the liberty of the individual."

"It might help," the Judge said, sighing. "So far I haven't the vaguest idea what's going on at all." He straightened. "And how in the name of all that's holy did you manage to produce Joshua Freitas as a witness? I mean, it *must* be Joshua Freitas—the computer recognized him and that's why it blew up!"

"We Timescooped him." Nickles shrugged. "Short range. From the moment before Dr Waley's sword ran him through. We showed him his own corpse, and believe me, that had a *very* sobering effect on him. It's going to be years, and I have psychiatric testimony to prove it, before he again thinks in terms of defending his honor by force of arms."

Judge Bushmill let his hands fall to his sides. He said bitterly, "I should have thought of that. All right, go on."

"Well, our aim is purely and simply to protect our various clients from indefinite incarceration," Nickles said. "Accordingly, we've organized guarantors for them all, who will stand surety to the maximum the court is likely to demand and warrant their future good behavior. If necessary, I can start a very fine hare running along the lines of 'guilt by association,' but I hope I shan't have to make use of it.

"Let's see now." He pulled a pad of notes from his pocket. "Ah, yes. Now the guarantor for Miss Tabitha Freitas will be the Hemisphere Joint Services Intelligence Agency, at the special request of General Fritz Wallington of the Aerospace Force. Apparently he believes that her particular techniques of infiltration and subversion will be of great value in future training programs, and wishes to test them for himself at the earliest possible moment with a view to her eventually undertaking a wide-ranging schedule of individual tuition at HJSIA headquarters. Then . . ." He hesitated. "Well—ah—psychoportrayal of the Earl of Winchelsea has indicated that he would be especially at home in such a context as is represented by the D.A.R., and the D.A.R. agree, for reasons I doubt if I need go into. Sieur Bohun de Freitas is beyond doubt the most experienced person at present on the planet where such matters as hunting, hawking and conflict with personal weapons such as the axe are concerned. You presumably know that Chief Rocket Bomb of the Seshawawa tribe has been working for years to restore the ancient values to his people, and he is extremely eager to benefit from the advice and information Sieur Bohun can offer them.

"Then there's Sir Godwin. Here we run into a rather curious legal anomaly, which the British Embassy has indicated its intention of exploiting to the utmost. Apparently a person born in his day, in their view, should not be subjected to the retrospective effects of subsequent legislation. English law in his time demanded that a man be tried by a jury of his peers on any legal charge whatsoever, and since he is a knight of the realm, you can see you'd be provoking a major diplomatic incident here, at the least. However, they will be extremely happy to stand guarantors for him and thus avoid the direct confrontation. As for the Reverend Ebenezer: the Combined Churches have long been hoping for a chance to get back to the original simplicity of the faith which their progenitors brought across the Atlantic, and it is my understanding that all their many member churches are eager to benefit from this first-hand contact with the purity and uncontaminated commitment which obtained in his time.

"Then there's the matter of Buffalo Hank, of course, and as far as he's concerned, the New Reformed . . . et cetera . . . Mosque of Islam, Incorporated, feel that it would be discrimination of the nastiest kind were he not to be permitted to share with their members his personal expertise in the kind of operation they have long been planning, to wit the engenderment of self-respect in their members by means of personal armed conflict, sabotage, and other manly pastimes. They are very anxious indeed that they should be allowed to learn at firsthand what Buffalo Hank can teach them, and failing your agreement, they have threatened to take the matter to the World Court."

"Oh, my goodness!" Judge Bushmill groaned. "Is that the lot?"

"Not quite. There remains Horatio Freitas. But it so happens that, since his arrival in the twenty-first century, he has become convinced that his terrors concerning the attempts of British agents to murder him were the result of nonphysical influences—that he was, in short, the victim of psychic forces. Count Alfonso de Freitas de Aragon y de Harpalus is tremendously interested in this and wishes very much to study him in person—on the Moon."

He thrust his notes back in his pocket. "That leaves Edgar Freitas, but his behavior has been so impeccable and his appearance on three-vee provoked such a favorable reaction among the public, we felt it hardly worth giving him legal representation. He has already, I'm told, applied for an officer cadetship in the Aerospace Force with a view to visiting Mars, Ganymede, and, if possible, the Pluto Orbital Station."

The Judge thought in silence for a moment. Then he rose with a determined expression. He said, "I'm going to deny the injunction. I'm furthermore going to have it recorded that the police application is unsupported by the evidence presented. And I hope sincerely and fervently that will be the end of it as far as I'm concerned."

He gathered his gown about him and headed for the door of the robing room. "Come on, back in court! Whether they've cleared away the rubble or not, I'm going to get out from under this mess right now!"

CHAPTER XXIV

"Congratulations, Chester!" Harold said, clasping the scientist's hand warmly and raising his voice to make himself heard above the hubbub of the celebration party that was being held in his Los Angeles penthouse. "I can't begin to tell you how sorry I am that you had to undergo that awful experience, and when I heard that all charges against you were being dropped, I was delighted!"

"Oh, come now," Chester said mildly, "it's nothing to make such a song and dance about. They dropped the charges for the good and sufficient reason that, within the time laid down by the Statute of Limitations, the experts said there was no hope of preparing, testing and deploying a legal computer that could handle the paradox implicit in having the man who was supposed to have been murdered take the witness stand and speak for the defense."

He helped himself to a drink and a canapé off a dumbwaiter as it floated past on its hissing cushion of air, and continued: "In any case, I really feel rather obliged to you."

"What?"

"Yes, I mean that." Chester sipped his drink and gave an approving nod. "A few weeks ago, you know, I was all set to resign from Freitas Interplanetary because the Timescoop project, to which I'd devoted so much time and effort, was being—in my view—treated as nothing more than a silly publicity gimmick."

"I don't blame you," Harold said. "It was about the most idiotic thing I ever did, dreaming up that family-reunion notion."

"I'm not sorry you did, not any more. I mean, as a result of that, I got the chance that Sparky says I'd been subconsciously hoping for all my life. I got back at a slave trader. I know I did, and I can look forward to remembering the fact for the rest of my life. What's more, that same slave trader was shown his own dead body, and oh, boy! Did that ever cause him to think furiously!"

"I imagine it should," Harold agreed, and suppressed a shiver.

"Oh, it did! You know he came looking for me and gave me the handsomest apology I ever heard from anyone? He was almost licking the floor!"

He glanced around. "Is he here tonight?"

"Yes, of course. But he's not wearing a sword any more. He's not even wearing the costume of his period. He says he wants to forget he ever graced the high society of Bath and find something to do with his new lease on life. Gambling, dueling and choosing smart new clothes, he's decided, aren't enough to justify a man's existence."

"Fine. Has it gone equally smoothly with all the others, then? I thought your lawyer Nickles did a magnificent job in Judge Bushmill's court, by the way."

"Yes, he did. He's around here somewhere too, of course. But—" Harold gave a wry grin. "I'm afraid the answer to your question is no, it hasn't gone quite so well in every instance. Let's see now—"

"You could start with Tabitha," Sarah said, coming up alongside him and taking his arm affectionately. "It turned out General Wallington is jealous, and so far they haven't reached a *modus vivendi,* but fortunately that's out of our hands now. Hmmm! But on the other hand, the Earl of Winchelsea is very happy indeed."

"You got the D.A.R. to take him on, I think," Chester said. "I didn't quite see the logic of that."

"Didn't you? Well, his specialty back in his own time was in masterminding court intrigues by playing on the susceptibilities of young wives whose husbands were neglecting them and spending all their time in politicking. We—or to be exact, Sparky—realized that an organization composed entirely of ambitious women would be his ideal element. And so far it's turned out fine."

"And Sieur Bohun is delirious." Harold grinned. "Finding that this sterile modern world of ours still had people in it who were bloodthirsty, keen on hunting and struggling to get back to what he thinks of as masculine occupations was exactly what he needed. He's just been made an honorary brave of the Seshawawa. Look!"

He pointed. Across the room Chester saw a feathered headdress towering above the crowd.

"Amazing," he muttered. "But I'll bet you didn't cope with Sir Godwin so easily."

"Funnily enough, we did," Sarah said. "You know what the British nobility are like these days—desperately trying to convince themselves that hereditary titles and so on are actually worth something."

"If that was aimed at me," Harold muttered, "I admit the justice of the charge."

"Oh, Harold, of course I wasn't aiming it at you!" Sarah squeezed his hand and smiled at him. "But it was a real shot in the arm over there for so many families with nothing but a title to mark them out to discover that they had a real live ancestor among them that apparently it's going to take him the next decade to accept all the invitations he's been given. He's taken care of."

"We—ah—applied a little pressure to Flannagan," Harold said. "It's absolutely astonishing just how many English noble families Sir Godwin turned out to have descended from him."

"I see!" Chester chuckled. "Very neat. Speaking of Flannagan, though: whatever became of this man who nearly upset the whole kit and caboodle—Detrick, who handed me that sword?"

"Oh, him." Harold dismissed him with a wave. "Solomon Schatzenheim changed his mind about giving him legal aid in the suit we brought against him for breach of contract. He has troubles, and I'm not at all sorry. Miriam is over there somewhere; you can ask her for the details."

"Poor Solomon," Sarah murmured. "He's the one I feel sorry for. He made the biggest possible fool of himself."

"I disagree," Harold said. "He didn't have to wind up the way he did; he could have prevented himself from being forced into this ugly mold of the big corporation boss which he accepted so cheerfully. He's not married to anyone—least of all Miriam—and he never will be. He married Four-S, and it was his own choice."

"Oh, never mind him." Sarah shrugged. "He's not a very cheerful subject to talk about. Look, Chester, there's Ebenezer over there. Have you talked to him?"

Chester stared around. "You got Ebenezer to a *party?* Never! You mean that's him, in the bright green outfit with the silver hair and the tankard in his hand?"

"None other." Sarah chuckled. "That's only the half of it, though. He's another of our failures, and my respectable cousin Adelina is furious with me, but it couldn't be helped. He deceived even Sparky, I think. Have you heard he's joined the Society for Absolute Orgasm?"

"What?"

"Truth," Harold said. "Sparky caught on faster than we did, Sarah dear—you must give him that. He suggested we have Ebenezer's head shrunk, and he responded magnificently. Within three one-hour sessions he realized that his attitude toward his wife and daughter was conditioned by his repressed incestuous desires, and decided to enjoy the opportunities which our more—uh—permissive age afforded him. The shrinker said it was the only analysis he'd ever conducted entirely in quotations from the Old Testament, particularly the stories of Lot's daughters and the fall of Sodom and Gomorrah."

Chester was about to say something else when he was interrupted by a rapid succession of banging noises. He said, "Don't tell me—was that Buffalo Hank?"

"Correct." Sarah gave a shrug. "I don't know whether you can call him a success or a failure, but certainly he's found his niche. You know it was his excessive fondness for women which led to his having to leave the East and head for the frontier country? Well, the idea of letting him train Black Muslims in hand-to-hand conflict and duplicity didn't work out too well, but exposure to a faith which permits a man to have four wives—*that* worked. Right now he has an American girl, a Canadian girl, a Swedish girl and a Nigerian girl. For variety. Last week he had a Mexican, a Hawaiian, a Latvian and a Japanese. Divorce is kind of simple in that tradition, as you probably know."

"But he's showing signs of strain," Harold said. "We

gather from Sparky that he's liable to work it out of his system by the end of the year and settle down. That'll be a relief; he's added more cousins-in-law to my family since he underwent his conversion than any six other relatives of mine in the whole of history."

Chester chuckled. "Let's see, that's seven of them accounted for," he said. "Where's your friend the poet, Sarah?"

"On the Moon," she shrugged. She turned away and took a fresh drink.

"Sorry, was that tactless?" Chester murmured to Harold.

"Not really. She's almost over it. But he's not the only one on the Moon, of course. Horatio is there, too, under rather different conditions. I don't think he much cares for Count Alfonso and his theories of occult control. But there's a blessing in disguise there: the shrinker we sent Ebenezer to says the best augury for the collapse of Horatio's paranoid fantasy is to find it less tolerable than the real world, and right now apparently he's about at the limit of his endurance. Once he stops being able to stand his own imagination at work, we can take him to bits and put him back together. He'll be all right in a few more months."

"Great," Chester said, and drained his glass.

"Harold, dear!" Sarah reappeared. "Chester, I'm so sorry but there are several staffers here Harold hasn't talked to yet, and I think he should: Helen, Louisa, Jimmy Quentin. Would you excuse us?"

"Of course. But before you go dashing off, one thing I did mean to ask: Harold, this first trial of the Timescoop led to so many problems—what are we going to do to turn it into a regular scientific tool? Have you figured that out yet?"

"Oh, we got a recommendation through from Sparky just yesterday." Harold looked smug. "We can finance William Shakespeare, Pericles the Great, and Julius Caesar on the basis of offers that have already come in, and the public-opinion polls indicate that they're people we can cope with. So that's our schedule for the rest of this year, and in the meantime Sparky has promised to sort out the ticklish candidates like Jesus and Mohammed. It's all under control!"

Hmmm! Chester thought about that last remark for a long while, fending off greetings and congratulations from other partygoers, and eventually managed to sneak off by himself in a corner where there was a phone. He sat down before it and punched for Sparky.

The unsleeping computer responded instantly and the Voltaire mask appeared in the screen. "Dr Waley!" the machine said. "A pleasure, believe me—I'm glad I was able to be of some service in extricating you from the predicament you found yourself in."

"Sparky!" Chester said sternly. "I think you planned this all along. Didn't you?"

He waited. There was an incredibly long silence. At the end of it, the gray and white image of the mask in the screen slowly turned bright pink.

"I blush," the computer said. "Still, I should have guessed that someone like yourself would have caught on. Do you mind very much?"

Chester hesitated. A smile spread over his face, and at length he shook his head.

"Good!" the mechanical voice said. "I'm sorry, of course—but can you imagine what it's been like to be the corporation computer for Freitas Interplanetary since Harold took over? I had to do *something* to make him start thinking for himself instead of relying on me all the time. It's so damned dull having an uninspiring mind at the head of the company!"

"I think you've cured him," Chester said.

"Mm-hm. So do I. And—" The computer sought for words in an absurdly human fashion. "And it's been rather fun, hasn't it?"

The immobile Voltaire mask parted its lips in a broad grin and faded from the screen. A distant voice said, "It might be better if you didn't tell the Freitases, of course."

For a long time after that, Chester sat contemplating the blank glass before him. But finally he said, addressing the air, "Well, it had to happen eventually, I guess. And we're still here."

He got up and went to find another drink.